BIGGLES AND THE SECRET MISSION

The first thing he saw was Gilmore, lying on the soft sand under the wing asleep. He seemed curiously still, ominously still, even for sleep. His position was an unusual one, too—more that of a person arrested in the act of stretching than sleeping, for his back was arched in an unnatural manner. Ginger could not see his face, but as he stared at him he felt a sudden unaccountable twinge of fear and shivered as if [illegible] draught of cold air had enveloped him.

'Gilmore,' he whispered.

The sailor did not move.

'Gilmore,' he said more loudly, a tremor cr[illegible] into his voice.

[illegible] the man did not move.

Ginger moistened his lips, and lifted his eyes again to the edge of the jungle.

This time there was no mistake. For a fleeting instant he caught sight of a leering face. Then it was gone.

BIGGLES BOOKS PUBLISHED IN THIS EDITION:

Biggles – The Camels are Coming
Biggles in France
Biggles Learns to Fly
Biggles and the Rescue Flight
Biggles Flies East
Biggles of the Fighter Squadron
Biggles – The Cruise of the Condor
Biggles and Co.
Biggles in Spain
Biggles and the Secret Mission
Biggles Defies the Swastika
Biggles Fails to Return
Biggles Delivers the Goods
Biggles Defends the Desert
Biggles in the Orient
Biggles – Flying Detective
Biggles – Foreign Legionnaire
Biggles and the Black Peril
Biggles Flies West
Biggles Goes to War
Biggles – Spitfire Parade (a graphic novel)
Biggles and the Battle of Britain (a graphic novel)
Biggles – Flying Detective (a graphic novel)

Biggles adventures available on cassette from Tellastory, featuring Tim Pigott-Smith as Biggles:

Biggles Learns to Fly
Biggles Flies East
Biggles Defies the Swastika
Biggles in Spain
Biggles – Flying Detective
Biggles and the Secret Mission

BIGGLES AND THE SECRET MISSION

CAPTAIN W. E. JOHNS

RED FOX

Red Fox would like to express their grateful thanks for help in preparing these editions to Jennifer Schofield, co-author of *Biggles: the life of Captain W. E. Johns*, published by Veloce Publications, Linda Shaughnessy of A. P. Watt Ltd and especially to the late John Trendler.

A Red Fox Book

Published by Random House Children's Books
20 Vauxhall Bridge Road, London SW1V 2SA

A division of Random House UK Ltd
London Melbourne Sydney Auckland
Johannesburg and agencies throughout the world

First published as Biggles Air Commodore
by Oxford University Press 1937

Red Fox edition 1994

3 5 7 9 10 8 6 4

Set in Baskerville Roman by Intype, London
Printed and bound in Great Britain by
Cox & Wyman Ltd, Reading, Berkshire

RANDOM HOUSE UK Limited Reg. No. 954009

Papers used by Random House UK Limited
are natural, recyclable products made from wood grown in sustainable forests. The manufacturing processes conform to the environmental regulations of the country of origin.

ISBN 0 09 939451 0

Contents

Chapter 1
An Unusual 'Whether' Report

'A penny for 'em.' Captain Algernon Lacey, late of the Royal Flying Corps*, looked across the room at his friend, Major James Bigglesworth—more often known as 'Biggles'—with a twinkle in his eye.

'A penny for what?' inquired Biggles, starting out of his reverie.

'Your thoughts, of course.'

'You're over generous; I don't think they are worth as much,' smiled Biggles.

'You seemed to be cogitating with considerable concentration,' observed Ginger Hebblethwaite, their protégé, who was passing a wet afternoon usefully by pasting up some photographs in an album.

'Since you're both so confoundedly inquisitive, I'll tell you what I was thinking,' growled Biggles. 'I was thinking what a queer thing coincidence is. I mean, I was wondering if it really is, after all, coincidence—as we call it—or whether it is simply the wheel of destiny spinning for a definite purpose. From time to time it makes contact with two or more people, or events. If they have no connection with each other the incident passes unnoticed, but if they are in any way related

*1914–1918. An Army Corps responsible for military flying, renamed the Royal Air Force (RAF) when amalgamated with the Royal Naval Air Service 1st April 1918.

the thing at once claims our attention and we call it coincidence.'

'Why this sudden transit to the realms of philosophy?' asked Algy casually. 'Is there a reason for it?'

'There is a reason for everything.'

'I see. I thought perhaps this perishing weather was starting a sort of rot in your brain-box. If it goes on much longer mine will start sprouting fungus.'

'I shouldn't be surprised at that,' returned Biggles evenly. 'Fungus thrives on things that are soft and wet—steady with that cushion, you'll knock Ginger's paste over. As a matter of fact, you are quite right. Something *has* happened, and since we've nothing better to do I'll tell you what it was. I've got a feeling—'

Ginger shut his album abruptly. 'Go ahead, Chief,' he prompted. 'When you get feelings it's usually a sign that something's going to happen.'

Biggles shook his head. 'I don't think anything will start from this,' he murmured. 'Still, you never know. But listen; I'll tell you. This morning, when I was going to the bank, who should I barge into but Tom Lowery. You remember Tom, Algy? He came to 266 Squadron just before the Armistice. He stayed on in the service after it was all over, and I haven't seen or heard anything of him for years. He's a squadron leader now, stationed at Singapore, so he hasn't done so badly. Naturally, we swapped *salaams**, with the result that we ended up at Simpson's for lunch. Now follow me closely because the sequence of events is important.

'While we were disposing of our steak and kidney pudding he started to tell me about Ramsay who, you

*Greetings.

may remember, was an ack-emma* in 266. [illegible]
a sergeant wireless operator mechanic—st[illegible]
service, of course. Or perhaps it would be more correct to say that he *was* a sergeant, because he no longer wears three stripes. Apparently Tom thought a lot of Ramsay, for not only did he wangle him into his squadron, but he used to take him in the back seat of his machine during air operations. Now during one of these flights Ramsay picked up a wireless message out of the blue, and Tom had just got as far as that with his story when who should walk in through the door of the restaurant, looking for a seat, but Jerry Laidshaw, who is now in charge of sparks** at the Air Ministry. Naturally, Jerry joined us, and after all the "well, fancy seeing you's" had been exchanged, he invited Tom to proceed with his yarn while he studied the menu card. So Tom carried on telling me about Ramsay. Is that all clear?'

'Perfectly.'

'Good. Tom, then, proceeded with his tale. Why he made so much of it I don't know, but I fancy he was feeling pangs of remorse on Ramsay's account. However, that's by the way. It appears that while they were in the air Ramsay picked up this message that I've already mentioned, and he handed it over to Tom as soon as they were back on the ground at Singapore. I can't remember the exact words, but the message—which was really an SOS—was to this effect. It was from the steamship *Queen of Olati*, and the wireless operator was broadcasting for help because they were on fire. He gave the ship's position, and concluded with the words "weather fine, sea slight". Now you'll

*RAF slang for air mechanic.
**Naval Slang: radio communications.

observe that the word "weather" occurs in that sentence, and upon that single word hung a power of mischief. Ramsay, in taking down the message—which came through, of course, in Morse—had spelt it w-h-e-t-h-e-r. Tom looked at it and said to Ramsay, "You should be able to spell better than that; you mean w-e-a-t-h-e-r." Said Ramsay, all hot and peeved, "No, sir. The word I took was w-h-e-t-h-e-r." Whereupon Tom told him to alter the message before it was handed in at the pay-box*. Ramsay refused. An argument then started which, I am sorry to say, ended with Ramsay losing his head and saying things which in turn resulted in his losing one of his stripes for insubordination.'

'But I don't see where there is any coincidence in this,' put in Algy.

'Wait a minute, I haven't finished yet,' replied Biggles impatiently. 'The coincidence—we'll call it that—is about to be introduced. This is it. As Tom finished telling me his story, Jerry, who had been listening to the last part of it with interest, blurted out, "But Ramsay was right! I picked up the *Shanodah*'s message at the Air Ministry, and the word weather was spelt w-h-e-t-h-e-r. I can vouch for it, because I made particular note of it." '

'At that, Tom gave him a queer look and said, "What are you talking about? I never said anything about the *Shanodah*; in fact, I've never heard of such a ship. I was talking about the *Queen of Olati* that went down in the Indian Ocean about six months ago." Jerry looked at him and looked at me. "Well, that's odd," he said. "I didn't catch the name of the boat when you were telling your tale, but when you mentioned the way the word weather was spelt I thought naturally that you were

*RAF slang for Squadron Office

referring to the *Shanodah*, which also—curiously enough—went down in the Indian Ocean, or the Bay of Bengal, which is practically the same thing. It would be—let me see—about five months ago. But she wasn't burnt. She hit an uncharted reef and went down with all hands." '

' "There were no survivors in the case of the *Queen of Olati*, either," put in Tom casually, and with that the conversation turned to something else, and no more was said about it. That's all.'

'Strange,' murmured Algy.

'Strange!' cried Biggles. 'I think it's more than strange when two mercantile wireless operators, both English and, presumably both educated men, misspell the same word—which, incidentally, is a word they must use more than any other. But when you add to that the fact that both ships foundered with all hands, in the same sea, within a month of each other, I should call it dashed extraordinary—too extraordinary to be either human or natural.'

'What do you mean?'

'Hasn't anything struck you?'

'No, I can't say that it has.'

'Well, this is the way I figure it out. The chances against two educated men misspelling the same word almost at the same time and place, and in practically similar circumstances, must be so remote as to leave one no alternative but to assume that they were both one and the same man.'

'But how could that be possible? The operator on the *Queen of Olati*, which went down first, was drowned.'

'He should have been, but there is something weak about that supposition.'

'Why not approach the shipping company and find out?'

'I have,' Biggles smiled. 'My confounded sense of curiosity was so intrigued that after I left Tom I went down to Tower Bridge and made a few inquiries.'

Algy threw him a sidelong glance. 'So that's where you were all morning, is it?' he growled. 'Well, and what did you discover?'

'That the name of the wireless operator was Giles, and that he was most certainly drowned. His next of kin was notified accordingly.'

'Why "most certainly" drowned?'

'Because his body was one of those picked up by one of the ships that raced to the rescue after the SOS went out.'

'Then that knocks your argument on the head right away.'

'It looks like that, I must admit.'

'What happened to the wireless operator on the *Shanodah*?'

'He was drowned, too; at least, he's never turned up, so he has been presumed lost at sea.'

'Then that must be the end of the story,' suggested Ginger in a disappointed tone of voice.

Biggles smiled mysteriously. 'Not quite,' he said. 'I was so chagrined at my theory all coming unstuck that while I was by the river I pursued my inquiries a bit farther. You may be interested to know that since the *Queen of Olati* and the *Shanodah* went down, two other ships have been lost with all hands—also in the Indian Ocean. Both sent out SOS's, but by the time rescuers were on the spot they had disappeared, leaving no trace behind—as the papers put it.'

'Was the word weather misspelt in those cases, too?'

'Ah, that I don't know. In each case the SOS was picked up by one vessel only. One of them was on the way to Australia, where she now is, but the other was homeward bound and docked at the Port of London this morning. She wasn't in when I came away, but she'll have paid off by now, and the crew gone home. Her name is the *Dundee Castle*, and the name of the wireless operator is Fellowes. Under the pretence of being an old friend I managed to get his address and his home telephone number from a very charming girl in the company's office.'

'You don't mean to say that you've got the infernal impudence to ring him up and ask him if the word weather occurred and, if so, how it was spelt?'

'That's just what I'm going to do—now. Pass me the telephone.'

'You're crazy.'

'Maybe, but my curiosity won't let me rest until I find out.'

'But suppose the word weather *did* occur, and *was* incorrectly spelt; what would that tell you?'

'A lot. It would be an amazing coincidence for two mercantile wireless operators to misspell the word they use most, but don't ask me to believe that *three*, all in the same locality, could do it. That is straining credulity too far.'

Biggles unhooked the telephone receiver and dialled a number. 'Hello, is Mr. Fellowes at home, please?' he asked. 'What's that? Oh, it is Mr. Fellowes. Splendid. Don't think me presumptuous, Mr. Fellowes, but I believe you were the officer who picked up the SOS sent out by the *Alice Clair* about three months ago . . . yes . . . that's right. My name is Bigglesworth. I've just been having an argument with a friend of mine about that SOS. The word weather . . . yes . . . quite . . . really! . . . Thanks very much. That's just what I wanted to know—good-bye.'

Biggles hung up the receiver, put the instrument on the table, and took out his cigarette case.

'Well?' inquired Algy impatiently. 'Out with it. Not so much of the Sherlock Holmes stuff. What did he say?'

Biggles lit a cigarette. 'He said that now I mentioned it, it *was* rather odd that the wireless operator of the S.S. *Alice Clair* should spell the word weather, in a meteorological sense, W-H-E-T-H-E-R!'

Algy thrust his hands deep into his trouser pockets and stared at Biggles for a moment in silence. 'By the anti-clockwise propeller of Icarus! That certainly is a most amazing coincidence,' he got out at last.

'Coincidence my foot,' snorted Biggles. 'There's no coincidence about it. It's a bag of diamonds to a dud half-crown that those three messages were sent out by the same man.'

'But that isn't possible—'

'Of course it isn't. That's what worries me. How can an impossibility become possible? There is only one answer to that. The impossible is not, in fact, impossible at all. Work that out for yourself.'

'But how could three men, miles away from each other, and two of them dead, be one and the same?'

Biggles shook his head sadly. 'Don't ask me,' he murmured. 'I'm no good at riddles. There's just one more thing I should like to know, though.'

'What's that?'

'Just what cargo those ships were carrying.'

'Why not ask Colonel Raymond at Scotland Yard? I don't suppose he'd know offhand, but he'd jolly soon find out for you if you asked him.'

'That's a good idea! Let's try. What's the time? Four o'clock. He won't have left the office yet.' Biggles reached for the phone again and dialled Police Headquarters at Scotland Yard.

'Colonel Raymond, please,' he told the operator at the Yard switchboard. 'Name? Major Biggleswoth . . . that's right.'

'Ah! Is that you, sir?' he went on a moment later. 'Yes, it's Biggleswoth here. I've an unusual question to ask, but I've a reason for it or I wouldn't bother you. It is this. Within the last six months four ships have sunk with all hands in the Indian Ocean. One by fire, one by fouling a reef . . . what's that? You know all about it! Fine! Then you can no doubt quench my curiosity. What was on their bills of lading?'

The others saw his expression change suddenly. From casual curiosity it became deadly serious.

'Really,' he said at last. 'What? No, I don't know anything about it. Why did I ask? Oh, well, just a hunch, you know—no, perhaps it wasn't a hunch. I—no, I'd better not say anything over the phone. What about slipping round here for a cup of tea; it's only a few minutes . . . Good . . . that's fine. See you presently, then.'

Biggles hung up the receiver and eyed the others gravely. 'It looks to me,' he said slowly, 'as if we may have hit a very grim nail somewhere very close to the top of its sinister head. The *Queen of Olati* was outward bound for Melbourne, loaded chock-a-block with military aeroplanes for the Australian government. With her went down one of our leading aircraft designers and a member of the Air Council. The *Shanodah* was bound for Singapore with twenty Rolls-Royce Kestrel engines, spare parts, machine-guns, and small arms ammunition. The *Alice Clair* was bound for Shanghai with munitions for the British volunteer forces there; and the other ship—the fourth, which we haven't investigated—was coming home from Madras with a lot of bar gold. Raymond is on his way here now.'

A low whistle escaped Algy's lips. 'By gosh! There's a fishy smell about that,' he said softly.

'Fishy! It smells to me so strongly of fish, bad fish, too, that—but I believe that's Raymond at the door. Ginger, slip down and ask Mrs. Symes to let us have tea for four right away.'

A minute later Colonel Raymond walked into the room.

'Nice to see you all again,' he smiled, after shaking hands all round. Then he sat down and turned a questioning eye on Biggles. 'Well,' he said, 'what do *you* know about this, eh?'

Biggles shrugged his shoulders. 'Nothing,' he said simply. 'I've been guessing, that's all.'

'And what have you guessed?'

'I've guessed that it would suit some people remarkably well if all British ships bound for the Far East and the Antipodes, with armament, never got there.'

Raymond stared. 'That's not a bad guess, either,' he said in a curious voice. 'By heavens, Biggleswoth, I always said you should be on our Intelligence staff. You're nearer the mark than you may suspect—a lot nearer; but how did you come to tumble on this?'

'And how did *you* happen to know all about it when I rang up? Shipping isn't in your department.'

'I was dining with the Commissioner and the First Lord of the Admiralty the other night. The Sea Lords are worried to death. So is the Air Council. But they know nothing—that is, they only know that these ships have disappeared. The public know nothing about these ships carrying munitions; naturally, we daren't let it get into the newspapers. But come on; this is very serious indeed. What strange chance led you to the trail?'

'Merely the fact that I have reason to suspect that the SOS sent out by each of the doomed vessels was broadcast by the same man.'

'Great heaven! How on earth did you work that out?'

'By so small a thing as a spelling mistake.'

Briefly, Biggles told his old war-time chief what he had told the others earlier in the afternoon.

When he had finished Colonel Raymond got up and began pacing up and down the room. Suddenly he stopped and faced Biggles squarely. 'Bigglesworth, if you'll give up this free-lance roving and join our Intelligence staff, I'll give you any rank you like within reason,' he declared.

Biggles shook his head. 'It's very nice of you, sir, but I should be absolutely useless in an official capacity,' he said slowly. 'I have my own way of doing things, and they are seldom the official way. If I got tangled up with your red tape I should never get anywhere. It is only because I've played a free hand that I've sometimes been—well, successful.'

'Yes, perhaps you're right,' agreed Raymond despondently. 'But tell me, have you formed any ideas about this business?'

'I've hardly had time yet, but my first impression is that some foreign power is operating against our shipping from a base in or near the Indian Ocean. They are sinking every ship which their spies inform them is carrying munitions to our forces in the Far East. Knowing that it is improbable that these ships could disappear without sending out any sort of message, they take control of the wireless room before the captain or crew suspect what is going to happen, tap out a false

SOS, and then sink her, taking care that there are no survivors.'

'But Bigglesworth! They wouldn't dare!'

'Wouldn't they! It is my experience that people or nations will dare anything if enough is at stake. You should know that. In the old days we had plenty of examples of it.'

The colonel suddenly snatched up his hat. 'I must get round to the Admiralty,' he declared. 'They must know about this.'

'What do you think they'll do?'

'Do! They'll send a flotilla of destroyers, of course, and—'

'Tell the enemy—whoever it is—that their scheme is discovered,' smiled Biggles, with a hint of sarcasm in his voice. 'Which should give them plenty of time to remove themselves from the scene, or look innocent when the white ensign heaves up over the horizon. Why not write to them and have done with it? You might just as well: the result would be the same; all you'll meet will be suave faces and pained protests.'

Colonel Raymond bit his lip. 'Perhaps you're right,' he said shortly. 'That's for the Admiralty to decide. You stay where you are; you'll hear from me again presently.'

'What do you mean, stay where I am?'

'What I say. Don't go away. Don't go out.'

'But I'm not in the army now. I'm a citizen and a free man,' protested Biggles indignantly.

'So you may be, but you'll jolly well do what you're told, the same as you used to,' growled the Colonel with a twinkle in his eye. 'I shall rely on you.'

Before Biggles could reply he had gone out and slammed the door.

'You see what comes of nosey-parkering in matters

that don't concern you,' Biggles told Ginger sadly. 'Let it be a lesson to you—ah, there you are, Mrs. Symes,' he continued, as the housekeeper came into the room with the tea-tray. 'Sorry, but we shan't have a guest after all. He was in too big a hurry to stay. Never mind, no doubt Ginger will be able to manage his share.'

'There now,' was Mrs. Symes's only comment as she went out again.

'Exactly,' murmured Biggles softly. ' "There now." We shall be saying the same thing presently, or I'm a Dutchman.'

'You think we've stepped into the soup?' suggested Algy.

'More than that. Before many hours have passed we shall find ourselves up to the neck in the custard, or I'm making a big mistake,' declared Biggles.

Chapter 2
An Important Conference

'If any one asked for my opinion as to the location of the enemy base—assuming, of course, that there is one—I should say that if you took this as a centre, and combed the area within a radius of a hundred miles, you'd find it.'

As he spoke, Biggles carefully stuck a pin into the big atlas that lay open on the table, and then glanced in turn at the others who were seated on either side of him.

The tea things had been pushed on one side to make room for the book which, lying open at a double page entitled 'The Indian Ocean and the Dutch East Indies', for more than an hour had absorbed their interest. Four red ink spots marked the last known positions of the ill-fated vessels, and from these lead-pencil lines radiated out to the nearest points of land, each line being accompanied by the distance in miles written in Biggles's small, neat handwriting.

'Mergui Archipelago,' read Ginger aloud, craning his neck to see the words that appeared on the map at the point which Biggles had indicated with the pin. 'What makes you think it is there?' he asked.

'Simply because it seems to me to be the most natural place,' replied Biggles without hesitation. 'It's the place I should choose were I asked to establish such a base for such a purpose. Look at the whole of this particular section of the globe, the Bay of Bengal, in or near which these ships went down. On the west it is bounded by

India. That can be ruled out, I think. What hiding-places does it offer to a craft engaged in a murky business of this sort? Very few, if any. Not only that, but India is a thickly populated country with excellent communications; a strange craft would certainly be noticed and rumour of its presence reach the ears of those whose job it is to watch such things. Admittedly, there are the Andaman and Nicobar Islands out in the middle of the sea. The base may be there, but somehow I can't think it is. If I remember rightly, the Andamans are used as a penal settlement for Indian political prisoners, and there are too many planters in the Nicobars to make it healthy for foreigners whose comings and goings would be bound to attract attention. Now let us go across to the other side of the bay. Here we have a very different proposition. Down the western seaboard of the Malay Peninsula there are a thousand places—creeks and estuaries—where a craft could lie concealed for months. The locals, such as they are, are very unsophisticated. Not only that, but the location is conveniently situated for the interception of ships bound for the Far East. They all call at Singapore, which is at the southern end of the Peninsula.'

'But what made you choose the Mergui Archipelago?' asked Ginger.

'Well, just look at it and consider the possibilities,' replied Biggles. 'Hundreds of islands—thousands if you count islets—lying at a nice convenient distance from the mainland—thirty or forty miles on an average—and spread along the coast for a distance of nearly three hundred miles. The islands are rocky, well wooded, with magnificent natural harbours. What more could a mystery ship ask for?'

'I've never heard of the place before,' confessed Ginger.

'Very few people have. I doubt if Algy and I would have heard of it but for the fact that we once flew over it for nearly its entire length, on the way home from New Guinea.'

'Are the islands inhabited?'

'Generally speaking, no, although I believe there is a strange race of Malay Dyaks, called Salones, who wander about from island to island in glorified canoes which they make their homes. Quite a bit of pearl fishing is done in the vicinity, chiefly by Chinese and Japanese junks during the north-east monsoon when the weather is fine and the sea calm. For the rest of the year, between June and October, when the south-west monsoon is blowing, it can be the very dickens, as a good many Australia-bound fliers know to their cost. We saw two or three junks when we flew over. Queer spot. Sort of place where anything could happen. Do you remember Gilson, Algy, that Political Officer who came to see us at Rangoon after the Li Chi affair?* I have a vague recollection of his telling me that the islands are infested with crocodiles and all sorts of wild beasts that swim over from the mainland of Burma and Siam. The thing stuck in my mind because he told me that he once saw a tiger swimming across, which struck me as most extraordinary, because the picture of any sort of cat swimming in water seems wrong somehow. But there, what does it matter? We aren't likely to go there.' Biggles closed the atlas with a bang and rose to his feet.

'Pity,' murmured Ginger sadly.

'Pity, eh? My goodness! You're a nice one to talk. What about that African show, when we were looking

*See *Biggles Flies Again*, and *Biggles Delivers the Goods* (published by Red Fox).

for young Harry Marton?* You jumped every time you heard a lion roar. Africa is civilized compared with this place. I—hello, who the dickens is this, I wonder?' Biggles broke off and reached for the instrument as the telephone repeated its shrill summons.

'Hello,' he called. 'Oh, hello, sir . . . It's Raymond,' he whispered in a swift aside, with his hand over the mouthpiece . . . 'Yes, sir? What's that? Dine with you? Delighted, of course. You want me to dress?** What on earth for? . . . Where? Oh dear! that isn't in my line . . . Right you are, sir, I'll be ready. Good-bye.' He hung up the receiver and turned to where the others were watching him expectantly. 'He's picking me up in his car in half an hour,' he said. 'Ever heard of a place called Lottison House?'

'Heard of it!' cried Algy. 'Great Scott! You're not dining there, are you?'

'So he says.'

'But Lord Lottison is one of the head lads at the Foreign Office.'

Biggles started. 'Jumping mackerel!' he breathed. 'Of course he is. I thought the name seemed familiar. It begins to look as if my confounded curiosity has got me into a nice mess. Well, I shall have to go and get ready.'

'Didn't he say anything about bringing us?' inquired Ginger, frowning.

'No, not a word,' grinned Biggles.

'Then I call it a dirty trick.'

'Never mind, I'll bring you a lump of jelly home in my pocket,' promised Biggles. 'I shall have to hurry. I've only half an hour to dress, and it usually takes me

*See *Biggles in Africa*.
**i.e. wear formal evening dress.

twenty minutes to get my studs into that boiled horror misnamed a shirt.'

Nevertheless he was ready and waiting when the impatient shriek of a hooter in the street below warned him that Colonel Raymond had arrived, so with a brisk 'See you later' to the others, he ran down the stairs and took his place in the limousine that had drawn up outside the door.

'You haven't wasted any time,' he told the Colonel, who, in evening dress, was leaning back smoking a cigarette. 'I wish you'd left me out of it. I'm not used to dining with peers of the realm, so I hope you won't accuse me of letting you down if I gurgle over my soup.'

'You'll find Lottison is a very decent fellow,' the Colonel told him seriously. 'This dinner was his suggestion, not mine. He's a busy man, and couldn't manage any other time.'

There was one other guest, and Biggles realized the gravity of the situation when he was introduced to Admiral Sir Edmund Hardy, head of the Admiralty Intelligence Department. Little was said during the meal, but as soon as it was over Lord Lottison led the way into his library, and without any preamble embarked on the problem that had brought them together.

'Well, gentlemen,' he began in a clear, precise voice, 'I don't think there is any need for me to repeat what we all know now, although only suspected until Major Bigglesworth brought the matter of the misspelt SOS message to our notice. That gives us a clue, as it were—something concrete on which to work. Our munition ships bound for the East are not foundering by accident. If proof of that were needed I have it here in the form of a cable which I have just received from Australia in answer to one I sent when this wireless incident was first mentioned to me late this afternoon. The Master of the *Tasman*, the ship which picked up the SOS sent out by the *Colonia*, the fourth vessel to be sunk, reports that the word weather was spelt w-h-e-t-h-e-r. That, I think, settles any possibility of coincidence. What is happening on the high seas, and how it comes about that an unknown operator has access to British ships, we do not know. The question is, what are we going to do about it? It cannot be allowed to continue, but I need hardly say that any steps we take must be made with extreme delicacy. At all costs we must avoid a situation that might end in war, particularly if—as it seems—the enemy has already established a means of severing our Far Eastern communications. Now, Hardy, what do you suggest?'

The admiral studied the ash on his cigar thoughtfully. 'Well, I—er—that is—I'm prepared to do anything you like—on your instructions. I can't act on my own account, as you know perfectly well. If you're prepared to back me up and shoulder responsibility for anything that might happen, I'm prepared to go ahead and comb every sea-mile between Calcutta and Singapore.'

A worried frown creased Lord Lottison's forehead. 'I'm not anxious to take the risk of precipitating the country into a first-class row any more than you are,' he said frankly. 'If things go wrong, the government will be thrown out on its ear, and I shall be the scapegoat.'

Biggles fidgeted impatiently. 'May I be allowed to make a suggestion, sir?' he said.

'I should welcome one.'

'Very well, then, let us get right down to brass tacks,'

proposed Biggles bluntly. 'Our ships are being sunk. Some one is sinking them, cleverly, secretly. Clearly, we've got to hoist the enemy with his own petard and dispose of him in just the same way—cleverly, secretly. Do you agree to that?'

'Absolutely.'

'Good! Now this private war is being carried on either by a surface vessel or an under-water craft. Whichever it is, it must be operating from a base which is being fed with supplies from the country that owns it. As I see it, we can do one of two things. Either we can sink the ship that is doing the dirty work, or we can wipe out the base. But if we merely sink the ship the people at the base, although they may be upset, may put it down to an accident and simply get another ship and go on with the job. So it is better to smash up the base than sink the ship. But when the base is smashed up it's got to be done properly. If it can be done in such a way that no one is allowed to go home to tell the tale, so much the better. That's the game they themselves are playing. Not that that is vitally important, because the country concerned can hardly ask us for an explanation without explaining what it was doing with an unauthorized base, anyway. Still, it's better to avoid complications if it can be arranged.' Biggles paused.

'Go on,' said Lord Lottison, looking at him oddly.

'If you are going to be content with sinking the ship, or submarine, as I suspect it to be,' continued Biggles, 'surely nothing could suit your purpose better than one of the "Q" boats,* such as were used during the war. All you have to do is send a ship out to Singapore, and

*An armed ship, with guns hidden or camouflaged, designed to open fire suddenly on an enemy vessel without warning.

let it be known that she is carrying munitions. Man the ship with naval ratings and line her sides with concealed guns so that the raider can be given its *quietus** as soon as it shows up.'

'Yes, that could be done,' declared the admiral, almost eagerly.

'The only drawback to the scheme is that it might only half answer the question,' observed Biggles. 'It isn't much use killing a wasp and leaving the nest. And, with all due respect to you, sir—' Biggles glanced at the admiral—'the finding of that nest might be a job beyond your power, because it is pretty certain that the enemy will know what you're after as soon as your ships start nosing about in unusual places. In short, it's a job for aircraft.'

'Then we shall have to call the Air Force in,' declared Lord Lottison.

'They'd do the job all right,' admitted Biggles, 'but they'd be up against the same difficulty as the Navy. The enemy would know what was afoot. Moreover, you would have to take a lot of people into your confidence. You can't send out several aeroplanes to look for something without telling the crews what to look for. And if you tell the crews, every one on the station will soon know, and it will only be a question of time before rumours reach the ears of the people we are up against.'

'Then what the devil *are* we to do?' burst out Lord Lottison irritably.

Biggles raised his eyebrows. 'Are you asking me that as a serious question, sir?' he inquired.

'You're an airman—something more than an airman, judging by what Raymond here tells me—

*Latin: its death blow.

so any suggestion you make will receive our earnest consideration. That, frankly, is why you're here.'

'Very good, sir. I was half prepared for this, so I've given the matter some thought, and this is my idea. It is a case where co-operation is necessary, but the co-operation has got to be worked in such a way that the fewest possible people know what is actually in the wind. The chief properties required would be an ordinary merchant ship, a destroyer, and an aircraft. The purpose of the ship would be to act as a bait, a decoy. No one on board except the captain and the wireless operator need know that. The wireless operator would have to know because it would be necessary for him to keep in touch with the destroyer and the aircraft, in code, on a special wave-length. The enemy also has wireless, remember. Our decoy ship would, to all intents and purposes, be engaged on an ordinary job of work. The destroyer would primarily be nothing more than a supply ship for the aeroplane, although naturally it might be called in to do any other job that became necessary. Have I made myself clear so far?'

'Quite. Go on.'

'The destroyer, one of an old type for preference, to lessen the chances of its attracting attention, will keep close enough to the decoy ship to be effective in emergency, yet far enough away not to be associated with it. The aeroplane will operate between the two.'

'But surely the aircraft would be heard by the enemy?' put in the admiral quickly.

'I hadn't overlooked that possibility,' replied Biggles. 'The aircraft will be fitted with one of the new silencers now under experiment at Farnborough.'

'How the dickens did you learn of that?' cried Lord Lottison aghast.

'I know a lot of things I'm not supposed to,'

answered Biggles imperturbably. 'As a matter of detail, the inventor sought my opinion on a technical question long before the device was submitted to the Air Ministry. But allow me to finish. Having equipped ourselves in the manner I have outlined, this is the order of progress. The decoy ship, its warlike cargo having been remarked in the press, will put to sea, followed shortly afterwards by the destroyer. Coincidental with their approach to the Indian Ocean, a long-distance flight will be commenced by a civil pilot. It is extremely unlikely that any one, even the most astute enemy agents, will connect the three events. That the pilot will encounter unexpected difficulties between Dum-Dum Aerodrome, Calcutta, and Batavia, is fairly certain, for it is all in accordance with the best traditions of long-distance flights. It is also extremely likely that he will be blown off his course by contrary winds, and possibly lose his way. Thus, no great surprise would be felt if he were seen *anywhere* in the region of the Bay of Bengal. Naturally, what we hope will happen is that the raider will attack the decoy ship, whereupon the wireless operator will report what is going on to the aircraft, or the destroyer, or both, who will head in that direction.'

'And sink the raider,' concluded the admiral enthusiastically.

Biggles looked pained. 'Oh dear, no,' he exclaimed. 'The skipper of the decoy, being prepared for trouble, should be able to avoid it. Having enticed the raider out of its lair, he will have to escape as quickly as possible. The aircraft will pick up the raider and note the direction it takes with a view to ascertaining the approximate position of its base. It is pretty certain to head for home after its attack has failed. And here let me remind you that if it *is* a submarine, submergence will not conceal it from the aircraft, for the pilot will be able to see it as clearly under water as if it were afloat. If the skipper of the attacked ship can give the pilot the direction taken by the raider, all well and good; if he can't—well, no matter, he will have to pick it up as best he can. From twenty thousand feet a pilot can see over an immense area, you know.'

'And if everything works out according to plan, and the pilot discovers the enemy base, what then?' inquired Lord Lottison curiously.

A peculiar smile flitted across Biggle's face. 'Well, the base will have to be obliterated—blotted out; otherwise there is no point in finding it, is there?'

'No, I suppose not,' was the thoughtful answer.

'How do you suppose the pilot will be able to effect the blotting-out process?' asked the admiral.

'He'll have to use his own initiative,' declared Biggles. 'He might be able to do it by borrowing a torpedo or a load of bombs from the destroyer. It all depends upon circumstances, but if he is a resolute fellow he'll find a way of doing it somehow. Naturally, he wouldn't appeal to you, or Lord Lottison, for assistance, because neither of you would dare to give an order involving the complete destruction of the property of a foreign power. He would have to act as an individual.'

'It sounds a very hazardous business to me,' murmured the admiral doubtfully.

'I don't think any one has suggested that it isn't, sir,' answered Biggles a trifle harshly. 'It's a matter of desperate cases needing desperate remedies, if ever there was one. Either we are going to wipe out this base when we find it, or we might as well stay at home. To be on the safe side—'

Biggles hesitated.

'Go on,' prompted Lord Lottison.

'Well, I was thinking, sir,' continued Biggles slowly. 'Supposing that when the pilot finds the base, for some reason or other he finds the job of destroying the whole works rather beyond him, he ought to be able to call for assistance.'

'How?'

'By asking an R.A.F. unit to come and do it. If they made a clean job there would be little risk of detection.'

'I don't quite follow that.'

'Well, put it this way. The thing might be made to look like an accident. After all, military aircraft carry out bombing practice regularly, and pilots are not to know that a secret submarine base had been established at the very spot selected for the bombing. What could the enemy do even if he was sure that his base had been deliberately bombed, anyway? You would simply look round, registering innocence, and say, "My dear sirs, we are very sorry, but how on earth were we to know that you'd got a lot of naval and military stores tucked away at so-and-so? What were they doing there?" What answer could they make? None, that I can see, without admitting their guilt. No, sir. If such a situation came about I fancy the enemy would have to take his medicine in silence.'

'By heaven, I believe you're right,' cried Lord Lottison. 'But tell me, who is to fly this aircraft you've talked so much about? Who could be entrusted with such a job?'

'Don't ask me, sir; I don't know,' returned Biggles promptly.

'There's only one man for the job,' put in Colonel Raymond quietly, speaking for the first time.

'And who's that?' asked Lord Lottison sharply.

'Biggleswort h.'

A smile spread slowly over the face of the Foreign Office diplomat, and he looked at Biggles good-humouredly. 'Why pretend, Bigglesworth?' he said softly. 'We all knew this from the beginning. The only question that remains is, will you undertake it?'

'Certainly,' replied Biggles without hesitation. 'If you can't find a better man, I can't very well refuse, even if I wanted to, the affair being a matter of national importance. But in order that there is no misunderstanding, I might as well say right away that I should demand certain—er—facilities.'

'Demand?'

'That's the only word I can use, since I would not undertake the job unless they were agreed to.'

'Well, let us hear them.'

'In the first place, I should stipulate that you gave me complete control of the whole expedition. It would be no earthly use my giving orders if they weren't obeyed.'

'Do you mean that you expect to be put in command of a destroyer?' asked the admiral incredulously.

'No; but the captain would have to act on my instructions.'

'But you can't expect a naval officer to take orders from a civilian.'

'It isn't a matter of what I expect, sir; it's a matter of what I should have to have. If the decoy ship, the destroyer, and myself, are going to act independently, we might as well wash out the whole project; you've only to look at your history book to see what has happened to expeditions when two or three people shared command.'

'But it's unheard of—a civilian in command of a naval unit,' protested the admiral.

'You can easily get over that,' smiled Biggles.

'How?'

'By giving me a commission in the Royal Navy, with rank superior to that of the skipper of the destroyer.'

The admiral stared. 'You're asking me to take a nice risk, aren't you?' he observed coldly.

'I suppose I am,' admitted Biggles. 'But what are you risking? Your appointment, that's all. I'm going to risk my life, if I know anything about it, and from my point of view that's a lot more important than your commission.'

The admiral glared, but Lord Lottison saved what threatened to become an embarrassing situation by laughing aloud. Whereupon they all laughed.

'I haven't finished yet, sir,' went on Biggles, looking at Lord Lottison dubiously.

'What else do you want besides a commission in the Navy?'

'A temporary commission in the Royal Air Force, with the rank of Air Commodore. You'd have to fix that up with the Air Council.'

It was the admiral's turn to laugh at the expression on Lord Lottison's face.

'It isn't a matter of personal vanity, sir,' went on Biggles crisply. 'I'm only thinking of the success of the show. I may need the Royal Air Force assistance, and what sort of reception do you suppose I should get if I, as a civilian, gate-crashed into the Royal Air Force headquarters at Singapore and demanded a machine, or even petrol or stores? I should be thrown out on my elbow; yet upon my request might hang the success or failure of the expedition. I've got to be able to get what I want without cables flying to and fro between the Air Ministry and Singapore. Let's be quite frank, sir. You wouldn't consider for an instant sending me on this job if there was any other way, or if you dared send a regular officer. But you daren't. You know you daren't, and I know you daren't; in case of failure or in the event of publicity—but I don't think we need go into that. I'm a civilian, and even if I had temporary rank it wouldn't matter what the dickens happened to me if things went wrong. You could have me hanged as a scapegoat if you felt like it, and I should have no redress. It might never be necessary for me to use my rank, but if I had it, instead of the delay which might prove fatal to the show, I should be able to walk into an R.A.F. depot, produce my authority, and demand what I required. Naturally, I should be fully alive to my responsibilities, and take care not to play the fool, or outrage the dignity of R.A.F. officers with whom I came in contact. It might be a good plan to warn the officer in charge of the Singapore station that I am about and that I might call upon him to undertake some unusual bombing operations.'

'Very well, if you think it is necessary I'll see what can be done; but by heaven, if you let me down—'

'Don't you think you'd better get somebody else to do the job, sir?' suggested Biggles coldly.

'No, no! No, no!' replied Lord Lottison quickly. 'You must see my difficulties, though.'

'I do, sir. I also endeavour to foresee my own,' answered Biggles quietly.

'All right. Then let us call it settled,' agreed Lord Lottison, glancing at the clock. 'By jingo, I shall be late; I've got to attend a Cabinet meeting at half-past ten. Draw up a plan of campaign as quickly as you can, Bigglesworth, setting down everything you require, and I will see to it that things are put in hand immediately. Will you do that?'

'Certainly, sir.'

'Good! We must break off the conference now. Don't forget to let me have that list.'

'You shall have it within twenty-four hours, sir,' Biggles promised as they all walked towards the door.

Chapter 3
In the Nick of Time

Biggles sat on a water-worn breakwater on the outskirts of the primitive harbour at Tavoy, in Lower Burma, and gazed pensively through the masts of several Chinese sampans, a junk or two, and other odd native craft towards the Bay of Bengal. It was a beautiful morning, with the morning star still hanging low in the sky, and that first false dawn, which is only seen in the tropics, bathing everything in a weird, unnatural light.

'You know, Algy,' he said moodily, 'the anxiety of this job is getting me down. I don't think I quite realized until we got here just what we have taken on. The world seems such a whacking great place, and—well, dash it, one feels that it's futile to try and control anything. And this job is so indefinite, not in the least like the others we've undertaken.'

Three weeks had passed since the momentous decision in Lottison House, and each day had been one of intense activity as plans for the expedition had been pushed forward. Unexpected difficulties had been encountered and overcome, but the unnecessary delays—at least, they seemed unnecessary to Biggles—inevitable when dealing with government departments, had made him tear his hair and threaten to throw up the project. However, in the end the preparations were concluded, and a general meeting of those chiefly concerned was held in an inner sanctum of the Foreign Office where, for the first time, those not acquainted with the real purpose of the campaign were informed and instructed in their particular duties.

Algy and Ginger attended in a secondary capacity in order that they might hear the plan unfolded in its entirety. The others present, beside those who had taken part in the preliminary debate in Lottison House, were: Air Marshal Sir Dugan Wales, Liaison Officer with the Air Ministry; Commander Michael Sullivan, R.N., Captain of H.M.S. *Seafret*, the destroyer detailed to act as a floating supply ship; Lieutenant Rupert Lovell, his Navigating Officer; Captain Angus McFarlane, of the *Bengal Star*, an old tramp steamer which had been selected as the decoy ship; and Chief Petty Officer Turrell, R.N., who was to act as the wireless operator on it.

Two speeches had been made, the first by Lord Lottison, who outlined the general plan in front of a huge wall map, and concluded by introducing Air Commodore Bigglesworth, the officer in supreme command of the operations. Biggles had, in fact, received a temporary commission with that rank from the Air Ministry, and notification of it had appeared in the *Gazette** under the broad heading of 'Special Duty'; naturally, the commission was to be relinquished at the end of the affair. He had abandoned his request for naval rank on the assurance of Admiral Hardy that Commander Sullivan would accept orders from him in his capacity of an Air Officer, the matter being made easier by the Admiralty 'loaning' the *Seafret* to the Air Ministry.

Biggles made the second speech. It was brief and to

*New Commissions, or appointments to a new command in the Army, RAF or Navy are officially published in the *Gazette*, a government newspaper for this purpose.

the point, and in effect merely a request for the loyalty and unswerving obedience to orders by which only could success be assured.

On the following day the *Bengal Star* put to sea, bound for Singapore via Calcutta. On mature consideration it had been decided that she should not carry munitions. Although a notice issued to the press stated that she was loaded with crated aeroplanes, actually there was nothing more romantic than good Welsh coal below her decks when she set sail. The *Seafret*, being faster, had given her two days' start, and another week had elapsed before the airmen set off after them with a prearranged rendezvous at Calcutta, from which point onwards the menace they were seeking might be expected to show up at any time.

The aeroplane they had chosen was a 'Storm' amphibian, aptly named *Nemesis*, fitted with two Rolls-Royce 'Kestrel' engines, and special tanks giving an endurance range of nearly three thousand miles. Personal luggage had been reduced to bare necessities in order that extra weight, in the form of a highly efficient wireless equipment and a powerful service camera, might not interfere with altitude performance. Altitude, Biggles claimed, was of paramount importance, for not only did it increase their range of vision, but it reduced their chances of being heard by the enemy; for although the special silencers had been fitted to the engines, there was no means of silencing the 'whip' of the propeller, or the vibrant hum of wires—both largely responsible for the noise made by aircraft in flight. A machine-gun of mobile type and automatic pistols completed their outfit, for with the *Seafret* in attendance anything else they required could always be obtained at short notice.

So far everything had gone in accordance with the scheme. The *Bengal Star* had proceeded on her way south-east from Calcutta, with the *Seafret*, in constant radio communication, following the coast but taking care to keep within reach should her presence be demanded. The *Nemesis*, in touch with both, officially on a long-distance flight to Australia, had followed in her own way, watching the *Bengal Star* from afar by day and lying at any convenient harbour during the night, refuelling when necessary from the *Seafret*. On two occasions, when the water had been dead calm, the airmen had spent the night on the open sea quite close to the decoy ship.

Biggles glanced at his watch. 'Well, come on,' he said. 'It's light enough to get away. Let's have another look at that chart, Ginger, before we go.'

He took the folded map which Ginger passed to him and opened it out flat on the breakwater. 'Now then, here we are,' he said, laying his forefinger on Tavoy. 'According to dead reckoning, the *Star* should be about here, and the *Seafret* here.' He pointed first to a spot about a hundred miles due north of the Andaman Islands, and then to a place much nearer the mainland, about fifty miles due west of the decoy ship's position. 'We mustn't let the *Star* get too far away from us,' he concluded as he folded up the map, 'although this cruising about all day and half the night gets pretty monotonous. I hate letting her out of my sight.'

'Turrell will always warn us the moment he sees anything suspicious, so I don't think there is any cause for anxiety,' murmured Algy as he moved towards the cockpit.

'That's true. In fact, that's my only comfort,' admitted Biggles, as he followed. 'It's the nights that give me the willies. We can't fly all day and all night, although we've jolly well nearly done that, but I'm always scared that something will happen when it's too dark for us to see what's going on. Start her up, Ginger, and then get to the keyboard and tune in.'

Five minutes later the *Nemesis* was in the air, with Biggles at the controls, heading south-west across the track of the decoy ship.

'What the dickens is Ginger doing?' asked Biggles presently, with a glance at Algy who was sitting beside him. 'He's a long time picking up the *Star*. You'd better go and see.'

Algy left his seat and went aft into the cabin. He was back in a moment, though, nudging Biggles impatiently. 'You'd better go and speak to him yourself,' he said in a normal voice, for owing to the silencers on the engines conversation could be conducted without shouting. 'He seems to be a bit worried about something.'

A frown of anxiety flashed across Biggles's face. 'Take over,' he said shortly and, leaving the joystick to Algy, ducked through the low doorway that gave access to the cabin.

Ginger was sitting at the radio, in the use of which he had had a concentrated course of instruction before leaving England, fingers slowly turning the tuning-in keys, but he desisted when he saw Biggles and slipped off his headphones. 'There's something wrong somewhere,' he said quickly. 'I can't get a sound of any sort out of the *Bengal Star*.'

'Have you spoken to the *Seafret*?'

'Yes.'

'What did they say?'

'They can't make contact, either.'

'Is that all?'

'Not quite. Lea, the operator on the *Seafret*, says he last spoke to the *Star* at five-thirty and got her position. Everything was all right then, and he arranged to speak to Turrell again at six o'clock if nothing happened in the meantime. Lea remained on duty, and five minutes to six, just as he was thinking of speaking again, he got the call-sign from the *Star*. It was repeated twice and came over very quickly as if it was something urgent. He picked up his pencil to take the message, but it never came. Instead, there was an uproar of atmospherics, or buzzing, that nearly blew his eardrums out. It went on for more than a minute and then cut out dead. After that there was silence, and he hasn't been able to get a sound since. He thinks something must have gone wrong with the *Star*'s equipment.'

'I don't,' muttered Biggles tensely. 'All right. Ask Lea for the *Star*'s last known position, and then send a signal to Commander Sullivan telling him to proceed at full speed to the spot. Let me know that position as soon as you get it.' Biggles hurried back to the cockpit.

'I don't like the sound of it,' he told Algy crisply. 'Neither Ginger nor Lea can get a sound out of the *Star*. No, don't move; you go on flying. Give her all the throttle and don't climb any higher; from this height we ought to be able to see the *Star* in about ten minutes.'

Ginger's face appeared in the doorway, and he handed Biggles a slip of paper on which he had jotted down the *Star*'s last position. Biggles passed it to Algy who, after a glance at his chart, altered his course a trifle.

Nothing more was said. The minutes passed slowly. Algy continued to fly, mechanically, depressed by a sudden sense of calamity that he could not throw off. Ginger remained in the cabin, still trying to make contact with the *Star*, while Biggles sat in the spare seat beside Algy, scanning the sea methodically, section by section, hoping to see the *Star*'s masts appear above the horizon.

Presently he glanced at the watch on the instrument board. 'She's gone,' he said, in a curiously expressionless voice.

'Begins to look like it,' admitted Algy, with fatalistic calm.

'Go on a bit farther,' Biggles told him, still hoping against hope that the *Star* had either altered her course or transmitted her position incorrectly.

But when another five minutes had elapsed they knew it was no use trying to deceive themselves any longer. The *Bengal Star* had disappeared.

'Let me have her for a bit,' said Biggles, and changing places with Algy, he began to climb, at the same time turning in wide circles.

Suddenly Algy, who had opened the side window of the windscreen and was staring down at the sapphire sea, caught Biggles's left arm with his right hand. 'What's that?' he said pointing.

Biggles, tilting the *Nemesis* over so that he could look down, followed Algy's outstretched finger. 'Wreckage, I fancy,' he said quietly, at the same time beginning to side-slip steeply towards it.

'It's wreckage, there's no doubt about that,' observed Algy, moodily, a minute later, when they were not more than a thousand feet above a number of miscellaneous objects that were floating on the surface of the tranquil sea. 'I think I can see oil stains, too. Is that a man? Look! Yes! By gosh! There's somebody there. I saw an arm wave. Down you go.'

'All right. Don't get excited. I'm going down as fast as I can,' replied Biggles, pulling the throttle right back and leaning over to see where he was going. 'We've only got to knock a hole in our hull on one of those lumps of timber to complete a really good day's work,' he added with bitter sarcasm, as he flattened out and prepared to land. 'Call Ginger to stand by to help you get him aboard,' he snapped, as the keel of the *Nemesis* kissed the water and cut a long creamy wake across its blue surface. The port engine roared, and the wake curved like a bow as the *Nemesis* swung round to come alongside the flimsy piece of timber to which the sole survivor of the ill-fated vessel was clinging.

'Look out! He's sinking!' cried Algy suddenly. 'I'll—' The sentence was cut short by his splash as he struck the water in a clumsy dive—clumsy because of the movement of the aircraft and the angle at which he had to take off to avoid a bracing strut.

He was only just in time, for the man had already disappeared beneath the water when he struck it. For a few seconds he, too, disappeared from sight; then he reappeared, catching his breath with a gasp, with the unconscious sailor in his arms. 'Quick!' he spluttered.

Ginger was already out on the wing, lying flat on his stomach, hand outstretched over the trailing edge. Still clinging to his unconscious burden, Algy seized it, and Ginger began to drag him towards the hull.

At that moment another movement caught Biggles's eye and he drew in his breath sharply. Cutting through the water towards the commotion was the black, triangular-shaped dorsal fin of a shark, the dreaded 'grey nurse' of the deep seas. He did not shout a warning, for Ginger was already doing everything in his power to get Algy into a position from where he might climb aboard, but in a flash he was out on the wing, drawing his automatic as he went. *Bang! Bang! Bang! Bang!* spat the weapon, as he opened rapid fire on the swiftly moving target. Whether he hit or not he did not know, but the killer swerved sharply and dived, showing its white belly as it flashed under the boat. Thrusting the pistol back into his pocket, he dropped on to his knees, and reaching down, caught the sailor under the armpits. 'You help Algy, Ginger,' he cried, and, exerting all his strength, dragged the unconscious man aboard. The weight on the wing caused it to dip sharply, which made matters easier for Algy who, with much spluttering and grunting, pulled himself up and then rolled over on to his back, panting for breath and retching violently from the seawater he had swallowed.

He was not a moment too soon, for as he rolled over on the wing the shark swept past underneath it, so close that they could see its evil little eyes turned towards them. It passed on, but the danger was by no means over, for under the weight of the four men the wing dipped down at such an angle that they were all in danger of sliding down it into the sea. Biggles dropped on all fours and began dragging the unconscious man towards the hull. 'Come on, Algy! Come on, Ginger!' he cried desperately. 'Get aboard, or we shall tear the wing off the hull by the roots. I—' He broke off, staring at a broad crimson stain that meandered along the wing and trickled away between the ribs to the trailing edge, from where it dropped into the sea. 'Great heaven! Where's all this blood coming from?' he cried in a horror-stricken voice. Then he saw, and shuddered. The unfortunate sailor's right foot had been bitten clean off above the ankle.

Biggles's manner was peremptory. 'Ginger, go into the cabin; make it snappy,' he said curtly. 'Get out the medicine box. I want lint, iodine, a roll bandage, and a piece of cord. We shall have to get a tourniquet round that leg pretty sharp or he'll bleed to death. Algy, get into the cockpit and take off the moment I've got him inside. Make for the *Seafret* as fast as you can and land as near to her as you dare.'

Half lifting, half dragging him, he got the injured

man into the cabin, where, on the floor, he applied rough but efficient first-aid. He was pale when he had finished, by which time the engines had been throttled back and the angle of the floor told him they were gliding down. He reached the cockpit just as the keel touched the water, and saw the *Seafret* standing towards them, not more than a hundred yards away. Clambering up on to the centre section as Algy switched off, he beckoned vigorously. '*Seafret* ahoy!' he roared. 'Send me a boat. Sullivan!'

The *Seafret*'s commander appeared on the near side of the bridge. 'What's wrong?' he called through his megaphone.

'I've got a wounded man aboard. Tell your doctor to stand by for an amputation case.'

Quickly the two craft closed in on each other; a boat was lowered from the destroyer, and in a very short time Biggles was standing on her deck while the wounded man was lifted by many willing hands into the sick-bay.

Commander Sullivan looked at Biggles's strained face and dishevelled clothing with anxious, questioning eyes. 'Where did you pick that fellow up?' he asked.

'He's one of the crew of the *Bengal Star*,' replied Biggles quietly. 'In fact, he's the only survivor.'

The naval officer blanched. 'Good heavens!' he cried aghast. 'You mean—'

'The *Star*'s gone—sunk—sent to Davy Jones; a few sticks and this poor fellow are all that remain. We saw him in the water, but a shark took his foot off before we could get down to him. Your doctor has got to save his life so that he can tell us what happened. I expect I shall be on board for some time, so you might get your fellows to make my aircraft fast and keep an eye on her while the rest of my crew come aboard. They are wet, so they will probably want to change. Anyway, we shall have to have a conference. I'm afraid my first effort at naval co-operation has not been exactly successful.'

Algy and Ginger looked at Biggles askance as they came up the steps that had been lowered and joined him on the quarter-deck. For the first time they saw him really agitated. His face was pale, his manner almost distraught, and his hands were clenched.

'What a tragedy! What a tragedy!' he muttered, pacing up and down. 'It's my fault; I should have foreseen it.'

'That's nonsense,' put in Sullivan, a good-looking fellow in the early thirties, tapping an empty pipe on the rail thoughtfully. 'You're no more to blame than any one else. How any one—ah! here's the doctor. Hello, Doc, how's the patient?'

The doctor's face was grave as he hurried up to them. 'He's conscious,' he said, 'but if you want to speak to him you'd better come right away. He hasn't long, I'm afraid.'

At the last words Biggles grew white to the lips. 'Hasn't long?' he echoed. 'Why, his foot—'

'The foot's nothing; I could patch that up. But he's got a bullet through the stomach, and with the water he's swallowed that's more than I or any one else can cope with. Come on.'

'You fellows had better stay here,' Biggles told Algy and Ginger, as he turned to follow the doctor and the captain down the companion. 'It's no use making a crowd, and I can tell you afterwards what he says.'

The wounded man's eyes were on them as they walked into the sickroom.

'May I ask him a few questions, doctor?' inquired Biggles.

'Certainly; I've told him I was fetching you for that purpose.'

'What's your name, laddie?' asked Biggles in a kindly voice, noticing for the first time that he was little more than a boy.

'Ladgrove, sir.'

'Can you tell us what happened this morning? Don't hurry—just tell us quietly in your own words.'

'Yes, sir, or I'll tell you as much as I know of it,' answered the dying man in a weak voice. 'It was my watch, and I was in the bows, on look-out, when it happened. It was just before six, I should think. Everything was still and quiet, and I saw what I took to be a fish about a mile to starboard. It was still dark, or, at least, it wasn't light, and at first all I could see was phosphorescence on the water, like as if it was a shark's fin or something. Then I see a thing like a pole sticking out and I knew what it was. I didn't see no torpedo, or nothing. I'd turned round, and was just yelling "Submarine to starboard" when there was a terrific explosion amidships. I believe there was two explosions, but I ain't sure about that because the first explosion bowled me over and I 'it my 'ead a crack on the deck. As I lay there I seem to remember 'earing another explosion. If I was knocked out it couldn't 'a bin for many seconds, because when I got on me feet everything was just the same except that we'd got a bad list, and fellers were coming up from below. I see something else, too. Funny, it was. The wireless aerial was a mass of sparks, blue sparks, like lightning darting up and down. Our engines had stopped, and I could 'ear the skipper blindin' the submarine to all eternity and shouting orders.'

The wounded man paused for breath, and the doctor moistened his lips with a sponge.

'What happened after that?' asked Biggles.

'I see some fellers start gettin' into a boat, but just as they were goin' to lower away, the *Star* she gives a quick lurch and threw the fellers 'olding the ropes all of a 'eap. The rope slipped at one end and threw everybody in the boat into the sea, the boat being 'ung up by the bows, if you see what I mean. With that the ship gives another lurch and starts to go down fast by the stern. I see the bows come up clear of the water and steam come pouring out of the ports. I thought to get a lifebelt, but she was going down so fast that I daren't stay, so I jumped overboard and started swimming as 'ard as I could. I'd got about fifty or sixty yards when I saw the sub pop up not far away. I see people come out on the deck and 'eard them talking in a foreign lingo. When I turned my 'ead the *Star* had gone, but there were two boats on the water. One wasn't far away, so I give 'em a 'ail and they picks me up. I don't know who was in 'er, because just at that minute the sub opened fire on us with a machine-gun.'

Biggles's nostrils twitched and he caught Sullivan's eye, while the doctor again moistened the dying man's lips.

'They fairly plastered us,' continued Ladgrove, 'and before you could say Jack Robinson the boat had sunk under us. I felt a bullet 'it me in the stomach somewhere, but it didn't 'urt much so it can't be very bad. I caught hold of an oar and 'ung on to it, and saw 'em deal with the second boat in the same way. Then for about twenty minutes they cruised round and round shooting at every one they saw in the water. They must have shot a lot of fellers that way, the murdering swine. Every time they came near me I sunk under the oar and 'eld my breath till I thought my lungs would burst. At the finish the sub made off, so I let out a 'ail or two, but I couldn't make no one 'ear. Then it got light and I could see that I was the only one left. I see the aeroplane coming and waved my 'and. A bit of luck it was for me and no mistake that you spotted me. I see that shark, too, while you was coming down. It had been 'anging about for some time, but I'd managed to keep it off by splashing, but suddenly the strength seemed to go out of my legs and I couldn't splash any longer. I felt the shark pull me under by the foot, and that's all I remember.'

'You've no idea what nationality the people in the submarine were, I suppose?' asked Biggles. 'I mean, you didn't recognize the type of boat or the language used by the crew?'

'No, sir, except that they seemed to be little fellows and rattled away like they might have been Japs, or Chinks.* Can I 'ave a drink, doctor?'

The doctor looked at Biggles. 'Any more questions?' he said quietly.

'Just one,' answered Biggles. 'Tell me, Ladgrove, did you happen to make a note of the course taken by the submarine when it went off?'

'Yes, sir, I can tell you that. It was due south-east. I know that because I watched it till it was out of sight, and it seemed to be going on a steady course.'

'Thanks,' nodded Biggles.

'I hope you're going ter get these blighters, sir,' called Ladgrove, as Biggles turned to follow Commander Sullivan towards the door.

'Yes, we'll get them,' smiled Biggles, and then, making his way to the deck, he stared with unseeing eyes at the blue water.

Ginger watched him curiously for a moment, and

*Slang: offensive terms for Japanese and Chinese.

then nudged Algy in the side. 'Don't tell me the skipper's crying,' he whispered.

Algy glanced up. 'Shouldn't be surprised,' he said moodily. 'I saw him do that once before, in France. Heaven help these skunks who sunk the *Star* if ever he gets his hands on them; they'll get little mercy from him now. Better not speak to him for a bit.'

The doctor joined them on the deck.

'I suppose there's no hope for him?' asked Biggles quietly.

'He's dead,' answered the doctor shortly.

Chapter 4
'Reported Missing'

Half an hour later, after a hasty toilet and breakfast, they all forgathered in the captain's cabin to discuss a revised plan of campaign made necessary by the loss of the decoy ship. It was not a cheerful gathering, for the fate of the crew of the *Bengal Star*, in particular the captain and wireless operator whom they knew, weighed heavily upon them.

'Well,' began Sullivan, looking at Biggles questioningly, 'where do we go from here? I can see you're a bit upset, which is not to be wondered at, so I'll take this opportunity of saying that you can still count on me to the bitter end.'

'Thanks, Sullivan,' answered Biggles simply. 'We've started badly, but we haven't finished yet, not by a long shot. I have only one fear, and that is that the people at home will recall us when they hear what has happened. As a civilian I could ignore such an order, but not as a serving officer—and a senior one at that—as I am now.'

'You'll tell them, then?'

'We shall have to. A thing like this, involving loss of life, can't be kept secret. Naturally, the public will not be told the truth, for that would warn the enemy that his scheme is discovered; but I think I can leave that to the discretion of the Foreign Office. I expect they'll break the news gently by allowing it to be known that the *Bengal Star* is overdue, and finally report her missing, believed lost. But she hasn't been lost in vain. For the first time there is a survivor to say what happened, and give us the direction taken by the enemy craft. You'll notice they've changed their plan. Instead of sending out a false SOS they contented themselves with jamming Turrell's equipment so that he couldn't broadcast a message. You remember what Ladgrove said about sparks flying up and down the *Star*'s aerial? That would account for the terrible noise that startled your own operator. It was the submarine soaking the air with electricity. The Germans used to do that in France, to drown messages sent out by artillery co-operating machines—but that's immaterial now. The chief thing is, we know the direction taken by the submarine, which give us a rough idea where to look for her, so the sooner we start the better. But first of all I think I shall run down to Singapore and have a word with the R.A.F. people there, to let them know we are about and that there is a chance we may need help.'

Sullivan suddenly sprang to his feet. 'By Jove! that reminds me,' he said. 'I'm sorry, but I forgot about it for the moment; I've a letter here for you.'

'A letter!'

'Yes, I picked it up at Akyab on the way down. It had been sent out by air mail, and the post office people there asked me if I had seen anything of you. They were going to forward it on to Singapore, but I told them I'd take it as I should probably be seeing you. Here it is.' He opened a drawer and passed the letter to Biggles, who raised his eyebrows wonderingly.

Tearing it open, he glanced swiftly as the signature at the end. 'Why, it's from Tom Lowery,' he cried. 'Lowery is an old friend of mine; he's a squadron leader in the R.A.F. stationed at Singapore,' he explained for the benefit of the naval officers. 'Pardon me; I'll see what he has to say.'

"My dear Biggles," he read, "This may reach you or it may not. If it doesn't there's no harm done, but having seen about your flight to Australia in the papers I thought it was worth trying. By the time you get this I shall be flying over the same ground on the way to Singapore. My leave is up, so I'm flying back the first of the new Gannet flying boats with which my squadron is to be equipped, and I thought there was a chance that we might meet somewhere. If you go straight on without trouble you'll be ahead of me, of course, but if you get hung up anywhere keep an eye open for me.

"By the way, I've been thinking about that conversation of ours at Simpson's. There's probably nothing in it, but a Chinese store-keeper in Singapore for whom I once did a good turn told me a funny yarn not long ago about something fishy going on in the Mergui Archipelago. Said something about certain people who don't like us very much having a wireless station there. I didn't pay any attention to it at the time, but lately I've been wondering if there was any connection between that and the message Ramsay picked up. Curiously enough, we were in that district when he picked up the message. Anyway, I mention it because, instead of flying straight down the coast, I shall probably fly down the Archipelago keeping an eye open for anything that's about, so if we miss each other that may be the reason. Still, we may meet at Alor or Singapore. Cheerios and all the best,

TOM."

'Have you seen or heard anything of an R.A.F. flying boat?' Biggles asked Sullivan casually. 'Tom is flying down to Singapore.'

'No, I haven't seen anything like that,' replied Sullivan.

'Never mind. Judging by the date on the letter he'll be in Singapore by now, so no doubt I shall see him there. For the moment we've more important things to attend to. Now this is my plan. I shall fly down to Singapore to-day and come back to-morrow. While I am away I want you to find a quiet creek where you can hide up, on the coast, opposite the Mergui Islands.'

'Why there?'

'Because if the submarine stuck to the course it was on when Ladgrove last saw it, it would make a landfall somewhere in the Archipelago. Anyway, that's where I'm going to start looking for it; and I shall go on looking while you have any petrol left. You may find it a bit dull just sitting in a creek with nothing else to do but keep me going with food and fuel, but I can't help that. Keep out of sight as far as you can; once the enemy know you're here our task will be twice as hard. That's all. If you can make a better suggestion I shall be pleased to hear it.'

Sullivan shook his head. 'No,' he said, 'I don't think I can improve on that. Looking for a submarine from sea level in this part of the world would be looking for a needle in a haystack, but with an aeroplane it becomes a different proposition. I have been here before, and I think I know a place where I can lie up with small chance of being seen. Here it is.' He got up and indicated a spot on the chart that lay on his table. 'If you don't get a signal from me you'll know that's where you'll find me.'

'Fine!' exclaimed Biggles, rising. 'All right, then; we'll get along to Singapore, and all being well we'll rejoin you to-morrow evening.'

The sun was sinking like a blood-red ball into the Malacca Strait when the *Nemesis* landed at Singapore, and Biggles, leaving the others in charge, wearing his new uniform for the first time, made his way to Station Headquarters, where he found a group captain in command, the air commodore being in hospital with an attack of fever. The group captain, who was still working in his office, looked at him curiously as he entered, and Biggles, rather self-conscious in his unorthodox appointment, lost no time in explaining the situation.

'My name is Bigglesworth,' he began, knowing that the other would perceive his rank by his uniform. 'You may have seen notification of my appointment in the *Gazette*, or you may have been told of it expressly by the Air Ministry.'

'Yes, I had a secret minute from the Air Ministry,' replied the other quickly.

'Good, then that makes things easier for me,' went on Biggles. 'No doubt you will wonder what is going on and what I am doing here. Well, I'm going to tell you. Frankly, if I obeyed my instructions to the letter, I shouldn't, but I think it's better that you should know because the knowledge will help you to silence any rumours that may get about the station. It may also help you to act with confidence and without hesitation if, in the near future, you get a message from me asking you to perform a duty so unusual that you might well be excused for hesitating, or even refusing to carry it out. Is that all clear so far?'

'Perfectly, sir,' replied the group captain, still looking at Biggles with an odd expression.

'Very well, then. This is the position. I'm on special duty. You probably know that, but what I'm going to tell you now you must never repeat except to the air commodore if he returns to duty. Somewhere in these seas an enemy submarine base has been established. Already it has sunk five British ships, three of which were carrying ammunitions. One, incidentally, was bringing you some new engines. I'm looking for that base, and when I find it I've got to wipe it out of existence. If I can find a way of doing that single-handed I shan't trouble you, but if I can't I shall send you a signal, and you'll have to do it for me with as many machines as you can get into the air. This is no case for half measures. You served in the war, I suppose?'

The other nodded, a light of understanding dawning in his eyes. 'Good,' continued Biggles. 'You remember the old Zone Call that we used to use to turn every gun in the line on to a certain target? If you get a Zone Call, beginning with the usual ZZ and followed by a pin-point, you'll act on it immediately. To make quite sure there is no mistake, the message will conclude with a pass-word, which will be "Nomad". On receipt of such a signal you will put every aircraft you can into the air with a full load of bombs or torpedoes, and blot the pin-point off the face of the earth.'

'Have you any idea where it's likely to be? I only ask because I must consider the endurance range of my machines.'

'I'm not sure, but I think it will be one of the islands in the Mergui Archipelago.'

'That's a long way; I don't think we could get there and back, with war loads, without refuelling.'

'That's a matter I shall have to leave you to arrange, but in emergency you can refuel at my supply ship. It's a destroyer, the *Seafret*. Sullivan is in command, and I'll tell him to signal his position to you so that you'll know where to find him. He's got about eight thousand gallons of petrol on board which you can have with pleasure, for by the time you've done your job we shan't need it. Have I made myself perfectly clear?'

'Quite, sir.'

'Then that's that. On, and by the way, if it becomes necessary for me to call you out you'll have to warn all your officers about secrecy. I need hardly tell you that no one except those taking part must know what happens. I shall spend the night here and go back to Mergui in the morning. Is Tom Lowery about? I'd like a word with him.'

The group captain raised his eyebrows. 'You haven't heard, evidently,' he said quickly.

'Heard what?'

'Lowery is missing.'

Biggles stared. 'Missing!' he ejaculated.

'Well, he's four days overdue. No one has seen or heard a word of him since he left Rangoon a week ago.'

'Good heavens!'

'We've made a search for him, but I am afraid he's down. If he's down in the jungle on the mainland there is just a chance that he may turn up, but there seems to be no earthly reason why he should fly overland in a flying boat. No, I'm afraid he's down in the sea.'

Biggles looked out of the window, thinking swiftly. 'I wonder,' he breathed. Then he turned again to the group captain. 'Perhaps your mess secretary* can fix us up for the night?' he suggested.

'Certainly,' replied the other promptly. 'I'll speak to him right away.'

'Good; then I'll be seeing you at dinner. Meanwhile

*An officer responsible for the running of the Mess—the place where officers eat their meals and relax together.

I'll go and see my aircraft put to bed,' answered Biggles, turning to the door.

Chapter 5
A Desperate Combat

Five days later, from twenty thousand feet, cruising on three-quarter throttle, Biggles and his companions gazed down on the sun-soaked waters of the Bay of Bengal. To their left, in the far distance, lay the palm-fringed, surf-washed beaches of Southern Burma, behind which a ridge of blue mountains marked the western boundary of Siam. To their right lay the ocean, an infinite expanse of calm blue water stretching away league after league until it merged into the sky. Below, the islands of the Mergui Archipelago lay like a necklace of emeralds dropped carelessly on a turquoise robe.

It was the fourth day of their search. Starting at the northern end of the long chain of islands, they had worked their way slowly southward, scrutinizing each island in turn, sometimes making notes of likely-looking anchorages, and sometimes taking photographs, which were developed on the *Seafret* and examined under a powerful magnifying glass. As each island was reconnoitred it was ticked off on their chart in order that they could keep a check on the ground covered, for with the number that awaited inspection it was by no means easy to commit them all to memory. Each day for eight hours they had remained in the air, but without result; and although they took it in turns to fly the machine, they were all beginning to feel the strain.

On this, the fourth day, they had seen nothing worthy of note except a junk that was moving slowly northward, leaving a feather of wake behind her on the flat surface of water to reveal that she had an auxiliary engine. Still proceeding on their way south, they reached the next island, a small one, unnamed on their chart, the first of a group of several, some large, but others no more than mere islets. Ginger was flying at the time, so Biggles and Algy were left to play the part of observers. Algy was using binoculars and, with these held firmly against his eyes, he gazed down at the irregular, tree-clad area of land which, from the altitude, looked no larger than a fair-sized wood.

Suddenly he shifted his position, readjusted the glasses, and looked again, while a puzzled expression crept over his face.

'Biggles,' he said sharply, 'can you see something—a speck of white, almost in the middle of the island?'

'Yes, but I can't make out what it is.'

'Try these.' Algy passed the glasses.

Biggles looked at the object for a long time with intense concentration. 'What did you think it was?' he asked at last, taking down the glasses.

Algy hesitated. 'The broken wing of an aeroplane,' he said. 'I thought I could just make out the ring markings on the end of it.'

'I'm inclined to think you're right,' replied Biggles quickly. 'We'd better take a closer look at this. Put her nose down, Ginger.'

Biggles studied the island inch by inch through the glasses as the machine glided down towards it, but there was no sign of life anywhere; in fact, the island was precisely thc same as a hundred others they had already looked at, consisting of a few square miles of heavily timbered slopes rising to a cone-shaped hill in the centre, the seaward side ending in steep cliffs, and the inland, or mainland, side shelving down gently to numerous sandy coves and bays which suggested that the island had once formed part of the continent of Asia. For the most part the timber was the fresh green of palms, casuarina, camphorwood, and broad-leaved trees, but in several places dark patches marked the position of mangrove swamps that are common features in tropical waters. One, larger than the rest, occupied the entire southern tip of the island.

At a little more than a thousand feet there was no longer any doubt; a crashed aeroplane was lying in the jungle about half-way between the eastern side of the island and the elevation in the middle, and the mutilated tree tops showed how tremendous had been the impact. One wing had been torn bodily from the machine and, impaled on the fractured crown of a palm, presented its broad side uppermost. But for this the wreck might have been passed over a hundred times without being seen.

Biggles now took over the control of the machine and landed smoothly in a beautiful little bay that lay at no great distance from the crash, afterwards dropping his wheels and taxi-ing up on to the clean, silver beach.

With firm sand under their feet they looked about them expectantly, hoping to hear or see some sign of the pilot whose accident had brought them down; but a significant silence hung over everything, and Biggles shrugged his shoulders meaningly.

'I think you'd better stay here, Ginger,' he said quietly. 'We may find something—not nice to look at. We shall have to leave a guard over the machine anyway. Keep your eyes open and fire three quick shots if you need help, although I don't think it will be necessary. Come on, Algy.' Without another word he set off in the direction of the crash.

Before they had gone very far they found it necessary

to draw the knives they carried in their belts, so thick was the undergrowth, and although it could not have been much more than a quarter of a mile to their objective, it took them nearly an hour to reach it.

At the edge of the clearing made by the falling plane they stopped, glancing furtively at each other, half fearful of what they knew they would find.

'I should say it's Tom,' said Biggles in a strained voice, pointing to the wreckage of a boat-shaped hull with the red, white, and blue ring markings of the Royal Air Force painted on it.

A cloud of flies arose into the air as they advanced again, and the details of the tragedy were soon plain to see. The pilot was still in his seat, held by the tattered remains of his safety belt, helmet askew, goggles smashed and hanging down. Biggles took one swift look at the face and then turned away, white and trembling. 'Yes,' he said, 'it's Tom.'

A second body, in air mechanic's overalls, lay a short distance away where it had been hurled clear, and Biggles pushed his way through the tangled wires, torn fabric, and splintered struts, towards it; the noise he made seemed like sacrilege, but it could not be avoided. A sharp cry brought Algy to his side, and he pointed an accusing finger at the dead man's forehead, where a little blue hole, purple at the edges, told its own grim story.

'That's a gunshot wound,' he said harshly. 'Tom was shot down. That is something I did not suspect. By heaven, if ever I get my hands on these swine they'll know about it. They're using aircraft besides submarines, evidently. Poor old Tom! Well, I suppose it comes to us all at some time or other,' he concluded heavily.

'What are we going to do? We can't leave them here like this.'

'Of course we can't, but it's no use our trying to do anything by ourselves. I feel we ought to take them to Singapore, but we can't do that without completely upsetting our arrangements. Perhaps there is really no point in it. I think we had better fetch the *Seafret* here and ask Sullivan to send a burying party ashore. Frankly, it's a task beyond me. I tell you what—you go down and join Ginger; take off, and as soon as you are in the air send a signal to Sullivan asking him to come right away. I'll stay and collect the things out of their pockets for evidence of identification, and then join you again on the beach as soon as you have got the signal off. How does that sound to you?'

Algy nodded. 'Yes, I think that's the best plan,' he said moodily. 'I imagine it has struck you that poor Tom must have gone pretty close to their headquarters—might even have spotted it—for them to shoot him down this way. I suppose he wasn't killed by a shot from the ground?'

'The bullet that killed the mechanic came out a lot lower than it went in; it could only have been fired from above.'

'Then that settles it. It's a good thing to know that the enemy have got a machine here somewhere. I'll go and get that message off to Sullivan; we'll see you on the beach presently. Don't be long; I've got a nasty feeling about this place.'

'I'm not feeling too happy about it myself,' replied Biggles as, with a nod in answer to Algy's wave, he set about his gruesome task.

Some time later, after he had recovered all the things from the dead airman's pockets, he made them up into neat bundles in their handkerchiefs with the log books and maps that he had found in the wreck. He heard the engines of the *Nemesis* start up, and, subconsciously, heard the machine take off; and half regretting the necessity for sending it into the air simply in order to use its radio, he was in the act of covering the bodies with as much loose fabric as he could find when he heard another sound, one that caused him to spring to his feet and stare upwards in alarm. Above the subdued hum of the 'Kestrel' engines came the sound of another, and the scream of wind-torn wings and wires that told a story of terrific speed.

He saw the *Nemesis* at once, climbing seaward on a steady course, just having taken off and clearly unaware of its danger. Behind it, dropping out of the eye of the sun like a winged bullet, was another aircraft, a small single-seat seaplane not unlike the Supermarine of Schneider Trophy* fame, painted red.

Breathless, he stood quite still and watched. There was nothing he could do . . . absolutely nothing. Except watch. And as he watched he realized that the end was a foregone conclusion, for the *Nemesis*, flying serenely on, was a mark that not even a novice at the game could miss.

In a sort of numb stupor he watched the pilot of the seaplane half pull out of his dive, swing round on the tail of the amphibian, and align his sights on the target. Indeed, so intense was the moment that he could almost *feel* him doing it.

At that particular instant the amphibian turned. It was only a slight movement, but it was enough to

*An international seaplane race competing for a trophy donated by M. Jacques Schneider. Britain won the trophy permanently by winning it three times in 1927, 1929 and 1931 using Supermarine monoplane racing seaplanes.

disconcert the pilot of the seaplane, who, at the same time, opened fire.

Biggles felt a cold perspiration break out on his face as the *Nemesis* swerved sickeningly. Whether or not the movement was accidental or deliberate he did not know, but when he saw the nose soar skyward and the machine swing round in a tight Immelmann turn, he knew that whoever was at the controls had not been hit, for the manœuvre was one that could only be performed by a machine under perfect control.

Again the seaplane fired, and again the amphibian twisted like a snipe as the pilot strove to spoil the other's aim. And for a moment it seemed to Biggles that he succeeded, although he knew quite well that such an unequal combat could not be prolonged. 'Go down!' he roared, well aware of the futility of speech but unable to control himself any longer, for his one concern at this stage was that Algy and Ginger might save their lives regardless of anything else.

From the behaviour of the *Nemesis* it almost seemed as if the pilot had heard him, for both engines stopped and, with propellors stationary, the machine began to zigzag back towards the land, at the same time side-slipping, first to left and then to right, in order to lose height. The seaplane was round after it in a flash, little tongues of orange flame flickering from the concealed guns in its engine cowling, and streams of tracer bullets cutting white pencil lines across the blue.

With a wild swerve, and with the seaplane in close attendance, the *Nemesis* disappeared from sight behind the high ridge of trees on Biggles's right, so that he could only stand and listen for the sound he dreaded to hear. He clenched his teeth as the harsh, staccato chatter of a machine-gun palpitated through the still air. It was maintained for several seconds, and then followed a screaming wail that was cut short by a crash like that made by a giant tree when it falls in a forest. Then silence. Absolute silence.

In an agony of suspense Biggles waited for one of the machines to reappear; but he waited in vain. The echoes of the combat died away; the parrots that had circled high in the air in alarm at the unusual spectacle returned to their perches, and once more the languorous silence of the tropics settled over the scene.

Biggles had no recollection of how long he stood staring at the ridge of trees, but suddenly he seemed to come to his senses. Throwing the things he had collected into a heap, regardless of stings, tears, and scratches, he set off at a wild run in the direction of the hill behind which the machines had disappeared.

Chapter 6
Jungle-Bound

In spite of their recently acquired knowledge that a hostile aircraft was, or had been, in the vicinity, nothing was farther from Algy's thoughts as he pushed forward the master-throttle of the *Nemesis* and soared into the air. As a matter of detail, he was not even thinking of the message they were to send, but of the dead men who lay on the hill-side.

Ginger, having already worked out the position of the island, was inside the cabin letting out the aerial, at the same time carefully forming in his mind the context of the signal he was about to send.

He had tapped out the call sign, thrice repeated, and his position, and was about to follow with the rest of the message when, without the slightest warning, the whole apparatus blew up, or so it seemed to him. There was a tremendous crash and, simultaneously, a sheet of electric blue flame flashed before his eyes with a vicious crackling noise, while a smell of scorching filled his nostrils. Temporarily half stunned with shock, he staggered up from the floor where he had fallen and tore the headphones from his ringing ears, only to be thrown down again as the machine heeled over in a vertical bank. As he clambered to his feet again a conviction took form in his mind that the aircraft had been struck by lightning, throwing it out of control, and he swayed through to the cockpit fully prepared to find Algy unconscious.

To his astonishment he found him very much alive,

crouching forward, but looking back over his shoulder with a terrible expression on his face. At the same time, above the hum of the engines, Ginger heard for the first time the unmistakable *taca-taca-taca-taca* of a machine-gun and, looking back over the tail, saw the seaplane.

Such was his surprise that for several seconds he could only stare at it unbelievingly; but then, his brain at last taking in the full extent of the danger, he turned and ran back into the cabin in order to get their own machine-gun from the locker in which it was kept. Ran is perhaps not quite the right word, for it is impossible to do anything but roll in a machine that stands first on its nose and then on its tail. However, he managed to get to the armament locker, and to it he clung with a tenacity of despair which the *Nemesis* performed such evolutions that he became convinced it could only be a matter of seconds before she broke up. The thing that worried him most was whether or not Algy had been hit. From time to time he could still hear the rattle of the seaplane's machine-gun, and the sound seemed to drive him to distraction. Bracing himself against the side of the hull, in a passion of fury he flung open the locker and dragged out the gun. Seizing a drum of ammunition, he clamped it on and, at imminent risk of shooting his own pilot, he staggered through into the cockpit in order to get into the open.

He knew without looking that the *Nemesis* was going down; the angle of the floor told him that; but he was not concerned with it. At that moment he was concerned with one thing, and one thing only, and that was the destruction of their attacker, the man who, he guessed, must have been responsible for the death of Tom Lowery and his mechanic. He felt no fear; he felt nothing but an overwhelming desire to destroy the man who was shooting at them; he wanted to do that more than he had ever wanted to do anything in his life before. After that, he wouldn't care what happened.

Actually, although he was unaware of it, his reactions were precisely those of scores of air fighters in France during the war; and they were the reactions by which those fighters could only hope to achieve their success, or even save their lives, for in air combat it is a case of kill or be killed.

Vaguely he saw the trees rushing up to meet them, was dimly aware that the engines had stopped. But neither of these things meant anything to him. He did not even hear Algy's frantic yell of 'Be careful!' With a fixed purpose in his mind, he scrambled up the back of the cockpit until he was standing on the hull just behind it, with the machine-gun resting on the main spar of the top plane. He saw the seaplane sweeping down over their tail; saw the pilot's helmeted head looking out over the side of his cockpit as he measured his distance; saw his head bob back and knew that he was squinting through is sights; knew that if he was allowed to fire at such point-blank range it would be the end.

As he glanced along the blue barrel of the gun a feeling of power swept over him, bringing with it a wonderful sense of satisfaction. Coolly and deliberately he trained the muzzle on the pointed nose of the other machine. His finger crooked round the trigger, pressed it down and held it down.

Instantly a stream of glowing white-hot sparks appeared. They seemed to form a chain, connecting the two machines. In a curious, detached sort of way he saw the drum slowly revolving, in funny little jerks, while his ears were filled with a harsh metallic clatter and his nostrils with the acrid reek of burning cordite.

The gun quivered like a live thing in his hands, but still he clung to it, his left hand clutching the spade-grip and his right forefinger curled round the trigger.

Suddenly the gun stopped moving; the noise ceased abruptly, and he looked at it reproachfully, unaware that he had emptied the entire drum. Looking back at the seaplane, he saw that it was behaving in an extraordinary manner. Its nose was dipping down—down—down, until it was nearly vertical. Why didn't the pilot pull out? The fool, he'd be in the trees . . .

'Ah!' Unconsciously he winced as the seaplane struck the trees and instantly seemed to dissolve in a cloud of flying splinters. The terrible noise of the crash came floating up to him, and he looked at Algy oddly, feeling suddenly queer. For one dreadful moment he thought he was going to faint, but the feeling passed, and again he tried to catch Algy's eye. But Algy, he saw, was not taking the slightest notice of him, or the crash. He was levelling out over a stretch of black, oily water, surrounded on all sides by trees with which he felt sure they would presently collide.

For a few seconds it was touch and go, and Algy only saved the machine by a swerve, before it had finished its run, that nearly sent Ginger overboard. Then, in some curious way, the *Nemesis* was floating motionless on its own inverted image, while little ripples ruffled the water and disappeared under the dark trees that lined the water's edge.

'Good shooting, kid,' said Algy, looking up at Ginger and smiling in a peculiar, strained sort of manner.

'I got him, didn't I?' muttered Ginger, as if he still had difficulty in believing it.

'You can write number one on your slate just as soon as you get back to where you can buy yourself one,' answered Algy, standing up and looking around. 'Did you get that message off, that's what I want to know?'

'No, I only got the call sign and our position out when a bullet knocked the instrument to smithereens.'

Algy grimaced. 'Do you mean to say that our wireless is smashed?'

'It's in so many pieces that it would need a magician, not an electrician, to put 'em together again,' declared Ginger. 'Why did you come down?'

'For two very good reasons,' Algy told him shortly, still taking stock of their surroundings. 'In the first place I wanted to, and in the second I couldn't help it. I don't know what's happened, but a bullet must have hit something vital. Both engines cut out together. I switched over to gravity but there was nothing doing, so I made for the only stretch of water within reach that was big enough to land on. I'd have got back to the sea if I could, but I hadn't enough height. Poor old Biggles will be in a stew, I'll bet; he must have seen the whole thing.'

'He'll be on his way here by now,' announced Ginger firmly.

'No doubt he'll try to get here, but from what I can see of it, it isn't going to be too easy,' murmured Algy anxiously. 'It looks to me as if we're in the middle of that big mangrove swamp at the end of the island, and there isn't a way out to the sea; I noticed that from the air before I put her down.'

'How are we going to get out?'

'I don't think we ever shall unless we can fix things up and fly her out. I wonder if we can make Biggles hear us? Let's try a hail.' Cupping his hands round his mouth Algy yelled 'Biggles' two or three times, but the only answer was the screech of startled parrots and parakeets that rose into the air from the surrounding trees voicing their indignation at the intrusion.

'Nothing doing,' said Ginger, and resting his hands on the edge of the cockpit he regarded the boundaries of the watery glade with interest not unmixed with apprehension.

On all sides the sombre mangroves lifted their gnarled trunks on fantastic, stilt-like roots from the black waters and slime of the swamp from which, here and there, sprang rank growths of orchids and other exotic flowers, the only spots of colour in a world of desolation and decay. Except for an occasional humming-bird, or butterfly of gigantic size, nothing moved. Even the air, heavy with the stench of corruption, was still, and endowed the place with an atmosphere of sinister foreboding.

Ginger shivered suddenly. 'I don't think much of this place,' he said. 'I should say it's rotten with fever.'

'There will probably be a mosquito or two about when the sun goes down,' opined Algy. 'Well, looking at it won't get us anywhere; let's see if we can get the engines going.'

It did not take them very long to locate the damage. The gravity tank had been holed, and the petrol lead that fed both engines from the main tank had been severed in two places by bullets. Several had struck the machine, but as far as they could ascertain nothing else was damaged except the wireless gear, which was completely wrecked.

'Can you put it right, do you think?' asked Algy, looking at Ginger, who was examining the fractures with professional eye.

'Yes, but it will take some time to make an airworthy job of it. I could make a temporary job with tape, but I don't think we'd better risk it; if the vibration shook the join apart again just as we were taking off over the trees it would put the tin hat on the whole caboodle. The same applies to the gravity tank. Much better do the thing properly. Lucky you turned off the petrol when you did, or we should have lost all our juice.'

'Lucky! You don't flatter me, do you? That was common sense. As soon as I smelt petrol I couldn't turn it off, or the ignition, fast enough. I was afraid the main tank had gone, and the thought of fire put the wind up me. Will it take long to mend those holes?'

Ginger glanced at the sun, now sinking fast behind the tree tops. 'I shan't get it finished in time to get out of here to-night,' he said frankly. 'Personally, I don't mind that; it's the thought of Biggles dashing about not knowing what has happened to us that upsets me. I wonder if it's possible to get out of this swamp on foot? I can see one or two places where the ground seems fairly firm. What with that, and by clambering over the roots of these foul-looking trees, one might be able to make terra firma.'

'How can we reach the trees?'

'Oh, we can easily fix up some sort of paddle or punt-pole. I wonder how deep the water is?'

A quick examination revealed that the stagnant water on which the *Nemesis* floated was not more than three feet deep. By splitting the cover of the armament locker and binding the ends together, they soon had a makeshift punt-pole, flimsy it is true, but quite sufficient to cause the lightly borne amphibian to move slowly in any desired direction; and as Algy poled carefully towards that side of the swamp nearest the place where they had left Biggles, Ginger got out his emergency repair outfit and prepared to mend the fractured parts.

'I tell you what,' said Algy suddenly, as the *Nemesis*

grounded gently on the mud in the shade of the trees. 'How does this idea strike you? I can't do much in the way of helping you and, as you're going to be some time, suppose I work my way to solid ground and look for Biggles? With luck I might be able to do that and bring him back here—either that or we could fetch you and spend the night on the beach.'

'I think it's a good scheme,' agreed Ginger. 'Whatever else we do, I think we ought to make a big effort to let Biggles know how things stand. But be careful what you're doing in that swamp; it wouldn't be a healthy place to get stuck in. If the going gets difficult you'd better come back rather than take any risks.'

'I think I can manage it,' replied Algy confidently, crawling along the wing and letting himself down carefully on the twisted roots of the nearest tree, regardless of the clamour set up by a number of monkeys that were catching their evening meal of crabs and limpets a little farther along.

'Got your gun?' asked Ginger, watching him rather doubtfully.

Algy tapped his pocket and nodded. 'I don't think I shall need it, though,' he said cheerfully. 'It can't be more than a couple of hundred yards to dry land.'

'I should say it's nearer a quarter of a mile the way you're going,' argued Ginger, as he turned to go on with his work.

For a little while he glanced occasionally into the swamp where Algy was slowly picking his way over the roots, but after he had disappeared from sight he became engrossed in his task and concentrated on it to the exclusion of everything else.

In such circumstances time passes quickly, and almost before he was prepared for it he became conscious that darkness was falling. Looking up with a start he saw that a thin miasma of mist was rising slowly from the silent water about him and, leaving his work, he leaned over the side of the hull, peering in the direction in which Algy had disappeared. As he did so he became aware of something else, although at first he could not make out what it was. Somehow the scenery seemed to have changed. Then he saw, and drew in his breath quickly with a little gasp of consternation. There was no longer any land visible, nor any of the tentacle-like roots. It was as if the whole forest had sunk several feet, allowing the oily water to creep up the trunks; so much so that the branches of the nearest tree, instead of being several feet above the wing as they had been, were actually brushing it.

Then, with a flash of understanding, he perceived what had happened, and wondered why he had not anticipated it. The tide had come in, raising the level of the water several feet.

'Algy!' he cried loudly, in a sudden panic as he realized what the result might be if Algy had not succeeded in reaching the far side of the swamp. 'Algy!' His voice echoed eerily away among the trees.

There was no reply.

For some minutes he stood staring into the gathering darkness wondering if there was anything he could do; then, with a little gesture of helplessness, he picked up his tools and carried them through into the cabin.

Chapter 7
A Terrible Night

Algy had not covered a third of the distance that separated him from dry land when he became aware of the flowing tide, although at first he did not recognize it as such and, as footholds and handholds became more difficult to find, he merely thought that he had struck a difficult part of the swamp, possibly a more low-lying area than the earlier part. But when he noticed suddenly that the turgid water was flowing steadily past him, gurgling and sucking amongst the hollows in the roots, he realized just what was happening. Even so he was not particularly alarmed, although he was certainly annoyed, knowing that his task would not be made easier by the new conditions.

But when shortly afterwards he saw that he could get no farther in the direction in which he was heading and, stopping to look about him, saw that his retreat was completely cut off, he experienced a pang of real fear, for he needed no one to tell him that a mangrove swamp is no place in which to be benighted.

For a while he scrambled desperately, often dangerously, from branch to branch after the manner of the renowned Tarzan of the Apes, but he quickly discovered that this method of progress was much easier to imagine than put into practice, as the palms of his hands testified. To make matters worse, he knew that he had been clambering about regardless of which way he went, taking advantage of any handhold that offered itself; and now, sitting astride a fork to contemplate his predicament, he was compelled reluctantly to admit to himself that he had completely lost all sense of direction.

On all sides stretched the morass. Above, a gloomy tangle of interlaced branches, fantastic, bewildering; below, the sullen water, as black as ink in the fast failing light except where grey, spectral wraiths of mist were beginning to form and creep silently over the surface. All was still. The only sounds were the soft, sinister gurgle of the questing water, and the ever-increasing hum of countless myriads of mosquitoes that took wing at the approach of night. The heat was intense. Not the fierce, dry heat of the midday sub, but a clammy oppressiveness that clung to the skin and made breathing difficult. Every now and then strange, foreign smells tainted the stagnant air: sometimes the noisome stench of corruption, and sometimes a perfume of glorious fragrance that seemed strangely out of place in such a setting.

He stirred uneasily, and in spite of the heat a cold shiver ran down his spine.

'Hi! Ginger!' he called, in something like a panic, and then waited tensely for an answer.But none came. 'Ginger!' he yelled again, but the only reply was the mocking screech of a monkey.

Looking down, he noticed that the water was still rising, for when he had lodged himself in the fork his shoes had been a good three feet above the level of the water, but now he saw with renewed misgivings that they were almost touching the surface. And presently, as he gazed downward with worried eyes wondering if he should climb higher, he became aware of a broad V-shaped ripple that was surging through the water towards him, and for a few seconds he watched it curiously, trying to make out what was causing it.

Straight towards the trunk of the tree it swept, and only at the last moment did a purely instinctive fear make him jerk both his legs clear of the water.

He was only just in time, for as he did so a long black object broke the surface and rose clear. There was a rush, a violent swirl, and then a crash like the slamming of an iron gate as the crocodile's jaws came together.

A cry of stark terror broke from Algy's lips as he scrambled frantically to a higher branch. Reaching one that promised to bear his weight, he looked down, but all was quiet again and still, except for a ring of tiny wavelets that circled away from the trunk of his tree and lost themselves in the gloom.

With every nerve tense, his heart thumping like a piston and perspiration pouring down his face, he again examined his surroundings for a possible way of escape; but with the water still rising matters were getting worse instead of better, and a few minutes' investigation proved to him beyond all doubt that, far from finding a way out of the swamp, he could not even leave the tree in which he was precariously perched. Swimming was, of course, out of the question, and as if in confirmation of his decision in this respect a huge watersnake, its head held erect like a periscope and its forked tongue flicking, went sailing past. He watched it out of sight, shuddering.

By this time it was practically dark and, abandoning all hope of getting clear until the tide went down, he was making himself as secure as possible on his perch when his hands, which were gripping the branch, felt suddenly as if hundreds of tiny pins were being stuck into them. Striking a match as quickly as his trembling fingers would permit, for the strain of his position was beginning to tell, he saw at once the reason: they were covered with thousands of the minute ants which, although he did not know it, were the dreaded *Semut apis*, the fire-ants of the Malay Peninsula. His lips went dry when, in the yellow glow of the match, he saw that the branch on which he sat was swarming with them; worse still, as far as he could see the whole tree was alive with them.

What to do he did not know: he was beginning to find it difficult even to think coherently. To stay in the tree and be eaten alive was obviously out of the question, yet to enter the domain of the horrors in the water was equally unthinkable. The burning in his hands ran swiftly up his arms and, driven to desperation by the irritation, he began to beat his arms against his sides in the hope of dislodging at least some of his undesirable tenants; but the only result was to bring down a shower of them from the branches above on to his head and neck.

Instinctively he started backing along the branch away from the trunk, which seemed to be the headquarters of the fiery army, but an ominous creak warned him that he was testing it nearly to the limit of its endurance. With his heart in his mouth, as the saying is, he began to work his way back again, but what with the irritants on his skin, the darkness, and haste, he missed his hold and slipped. He made a frenzied clutch at the sagging branch to save himself, but almost before he knew what was happening he found himself hanging at the full length of his arms with his feet only a few inches above the water. He could hear the branch creaking under his weight and, knowing that it would not support him for many more seconds, he strove with a determination born of despair to pull himself up again, performing extraordinary gymnastics with his legs as he tried to hook them round the branch in order to take some of the weight from his arms; but it was a feat beyond his strength, for the branch sagged lower and lower and eluded his ever groping legs.

The creaking became a definite crackle and, perceiving beyond all doubt what must happen within the next few seconds, he let out a yell of fear. It was still ringing in his ears when, with a loud crack, the branch broke off short, and the next moment, with a mighty splash, he, the branch, and the ants disappeared under the water.

He was up again in an instant, blowing and gasping, and with his toes curling with horror he struck out madly for the nearest tree. He could not have been more than a quarter of a minute reaching it, but to his distorted imagination it seemed like eternity and, clutching the rough bole in his arms, he went up it in a manner that would have been impossible in cold blood. Grabbing at a bough, he pulled himself on to it and, throwing a leg over it where it joined the trunk, he sagged limply, panting for breath, watching as in a nightmare the water dripping from him into the black stream below.

By this time he had reached that degree of misery that knows neither pain nor fear, a lamentable condition in which death appears as a welcome release; and it may have been due to this that at first he regarded a vague black shadow that appeared suddenly on the water a few yards away without any particular emotion. But as he watched it, knowing that although he could not see them two cold eyes were watching him too, a bitter hatred slowly took possession of him and of it a new idea was born. He remembered something. Feeling in his soaking pocket, he took out his automatic and, taking careful aim, pulled the trigger. *Bang! Bang! Bang!* Three times the weapon roared.

With a convulsive swirl the crocodile half threw itself out of the water, plunged back, and then disappeared from sight.

'Hold that lot, you ugly swine,' he growled viciously, as he stared down at the turmoil below him.

'Here, be careful what you're doing with that gun,' called a voice near at hand.

In his astonishment Algy nearly fell into the water again, but as he recognized the voice a little cry of relief broke from his lips. Peering into the darkness, he could just make out a queer-shaped mass moving smoothly over the oily surface of the water towards him. 'Hi! Biggles!' he called joyfully.

'Where the dickens are you?' came Biggles's voice.

'Here—up a tree,' answered Algy. 'What on earth are you in—a boat?'

'I'm not swimming, you can bet your life on that,' returned Biggles tersely. 'A lot of very nasty people use this place as a bathing pool, as you may have noticed. What in the name of goodness are you doing up there?' he concluded, as he drew up underneath.

'What do you suppose?' replied Algy shortly. 'I'm not practising a trapeze act or anything like that.'

'It looks uncommonly like it,' grinned Biggles, as Algy lowered himself down into the boat. 'Hey! Go steady; this isn't a barge,' he went on quickly, clutching at the sides of the frail craft as Algy let go his hold. 'What's happened to Ginger? Where is he?'

'The last time I saw him was in the machine, nailing up holes in the petrol tank,' answered Algy wearily.

'What machine?'

'Our machine, of course.'

Biggles stared. 'But I thought I heard it crash,' he

muttered incredulously. 'I've been looking for the wreck ever since.'

'It was the other fellow who crashed, not us. Ginger fairly plastered him with a whole drum of ammo from about ten yards' range.'

'Where did he crash?'

'Somewhere over the other side of this swamp, which is about the nearest thing to hell that I've ever struck. Did you ever see such a foul place in your life? There's a sort of lake in the middle of it, and I managed to get the *Nemesis* down on it. By the way, where the dickens did you get this conveyance? It feels kind of soft for a boat.'

'It's the collapsible rubber canoe out of poor Tom's crash,' replied Biggles. 'After running about for hours like a lunatic looking for a way into this confounded bog, I suddenly had a brainwave and remembered that nearly all big service marine aircraft now carry collapsible boats. I went back and looked for it and there it was, although there were two or three bullet holes through it which I had to mend. It isn't too safe now, but it's better than nothing. Is the machine badly damaged?'

'No. I had a petrol lead shot away, so I had to get down as best I could and where I could. The only place was the lake I mentioned just now. Then, knowing you'd be worried, I set off to look for you while Ginger did the repairs, but I got marooned in this tree by the tide. Where were you bound for when you came along this way?'

'I was looking for you,' answered Biggles, 'although I don't mind admitting that I was lost to the world. The whole place looks alike, and I fancy I had been going round in circles when I heard you singing—'

'Singing, my foot!' interrupted Algy indignantly. 'I was yelling with fright.'

'Well, it was easy enough to make the mistake,' protested Biggles, grinning. 'But let's try and get out of this. I'm not particular, but this strikes me as being neither the time nor place for a picnic. In which direction is this lake of yours?'

'I haven't the remotest idea.'

'Then we'd better set about looking for it. Hark! That sounds like Ginger,' went on Biggles quickly, as a revolver shot split the silence. 'He must have heard your shots and is trying to let you know where he is. From which direction do you think the sound came?'

'Over there.' Algy pointed vaguely into the darkness.

'I thought so, too,' declared Biggles, urging the tiny craft forward with its small paddle. 'We'll try it, anyway. Fire another shot and keep your eyes open for an answering flash. We ought to be able to see it in this darkness.'

Algy pointed the muzzle of his automatic skywards and pulled the trigger, only to cower down as a pandemonium of shrieks and barks instantly broke out over his head. 'What in the name of thunder is that?' he gasped.

'It sounds as if some of your pals up in the trees thought you were shooting at them,' murmured Biggles, moving the boat forward again as a flash showed momentarily through the trees some distance away, to be followed by another report.

After that it was only a question of time while they sought a way through the labyrinth of branches before they reached the open stretch of water on which the *Nemesis* rested; in the starlight they could see Ginger's silhouette standing erect in the cockpit, looking towards the trees. He let out a hail when he saw them.

'You've been a long time,' he observed, looking at Algy reproachfully as they drew alongside. 'I began to think you weren't coming back.'

'Curiously enough, I was thinking the same thing not long ago,' Algy told him meaningly as he climbed aboard.

'Never mind about that. We're here now, and that's all that matters,' murmured Biggles philosophically. 'Open up some of the emergency rations, Ginger, and let's have a bite of food. After that I think a spot of shut-eye is indicated. We shall have to be on the move as soon as it's daylight. If that fellow you shot down has any friends about they'll be looking for him bright and early. Besides, I want to find out where he came from.'

Chapter 8
Shadows on the Shore

'Whereabouts did the seaplane hit the ground, Ginger?' asked Biggles, shortly after dawn the following morning as, standing on the hull, he sponged himself down briskly from a bucket of cold water. They had already discussed the details of the combat.

Ginger, who was putting the finishing touches to the fractured petrol lead, pointed to an adjacent tree-covered slope that rose just beyond the irregular outline of the mangroves. 'Somewhere over there,' he said. 'Why? Are you thinking of going to it?'

'I don't know yet,' replied Biggles thoughtfully, drying himself on a well-worn strip of towel. 'The first thing I want to do is to get out of this place and find the *Seafret*; it's bad, this being out of touch, although you were lucky to send her our position before that fellow in the seaplane shot your instrument to pieces; still, Sullivan will wonder what the deuce has happened to us. When we find her, if we do, I may go and examine what's left of the seaplane while his sailors are ashore burying poor Tom and his mechanic—that is, provided the place isn't too difficult to reach. I ought to have a shot at it, anyway, because it may furnish us with some important information.'

'Such as?' inquired Algy, who was anointing his ant-bites with boracic ointment from the medicine chest.

'Well, it would be something to know for certain the nationality of the people we're up against, wouldn't it?'

'By jingo, it would! I never thought of that,' confessed Algy. 'What do you suppose his people will think when he fails to return?'

'I don't care two hoots what they think. I only hope they didn't hear the shooting or see anything of the combat yesterday.'

Algy glanced back over his shoulder to where Biggles was standing watching Ginger at work. 'Good gracious! Do you think they may be as close as that?' he asked quickly.

'I don't think they can be very far away or surely there would have been no point in their shooting down Tom's machine. What I should very much like to know is whether the fellow in the seaplane spotted us flying around from his base on the ground, and came out deliberately to get us, or whether he was merely cruising about and lighted on us by accident.'

'He may have been searching for Tom's crash,' suggested Ginger.

'That isn't at all unlikely,' agreed Biggles, 'although had that been the case one would have thought that he would have been flying very low, instead of high up, as he must have been or we should have heard him before we did.'

'I suppose it is also possible that he was sitting high up over his base, doing a sort of aerodrome patrol as a routine job, on the look-out for strange ships or aircraft, when he saw us a long way off,' went on Ginger thoughtfully.

'Quite possible,' agreed Biggles readily. 'He may have been doing that when he spotted Tom.'

'I fancy Tom must have been pretty close to their base—might even have spotted it—or surely they wouldn't have killed him.'

'Oh, I wouldn't stake too much on that,' declared Biggles. 'After all, there was no reason why he shouldn't be shot down. He was an enemy, assuming that all British subjects are regarded as enemies by these people, as presumably they are; and don't forget that there was little or no risk of discovery. Tom's machine wasn't fitted with guns; I know that because I looked particularly to see. No doubt the guns would have been put on the machine when he got to Singapore. The seaplane pilot probably guessed he would be unarmed, as there is no war on, and that being so his task would be easy. In fact, Tom would merely provide him with a useful bit of target practice, quite apart from enabling him to destroy another piece of British property. If these skunks are out to sink British ships, there doesn't seem to be any reason why they shouldn't be equally glad to smash up British aircraft. But there, what's the use of guessing? Tom's dead, and the fellow who killed him is dead, or it looks that way to me, so neither of them can tell us anything. I suppose there's no doubt about the fellow in the seaplane being killed, Algy?'

'None whatever,' declared Algy emphatically. 'I saw him hit the carpet and I never saw a worse crash. The kite went to pieces like a sheet of wet tissue-paper in a gale.'

'I see,' replied Biggles. 'All right. If you fellows are through we'll see about getting away. There isn't a dickens of a lot of room. Have you finished, Ginger?'

'Yes, I think she's OK now,' answered Ginger, stepping down into the cockpit and turning on the petrol. 'We can test her, anyway. I've put some juice into the gravity tank; it isn't full, but there's sufficient to take us out of this place if the main tank doesn't function.'

Decks were quickly cleared; small kit and tools were stowed away and everything made ship-shape for departure. Biggles took his place at the joystick with

Algy beside him, while Ginger watched proceedings from the cabin door.

'I hope she'll unstick,' muttered Biggles anxiously, as he twirled the self-starter, and smiled his relief as both engines came to life at the first attempt.

Twice he taxied the full length of the lagoon, both to ascertain that the engines were giving their full revolutions and to make sure that there were no partly submerged obstacles in the way; and then, satisfied that all was well, he turned the machine round facing the longest run possible for the take-off.

With a muffled roar that sent a cloud of birds wheeling high into the air with fright, the amphibian sped across the placid water, leaving a churning wake of foam to mark her passage. With a normally powered machine it is likely that the take-off would have ended in disaster, for the *Nemesis* was loath to leave the water; but the extra horses under the engine cowling saved them, and, although they had very little room to spare, they cleared the trees, whereupon Biggles at once swung round towards the open sea.

The first thing they saw was the *Seafret*, cruising along near the shore at half speed, apparently looking for them. There was a bustle on her decks as the aircraft climbed into view, and as he swept low over her Biggles saw her commander wave to him from the bridge. There was no point in prolonging the flight, so he throttled back and glided into the little bay they had used on the previous day, and there, a few minutes later, the *Seafret* joined them and dropped her anchor.

'What the deuce are you fellows playing at?' roared Sullivan, half angrily, as he ran alongside.

'Send us a boat and I'll tell you,' grinned Biggles.

A boat was quickly lowered, and the three airmen,

after making the amphibian fast to the destroyer, joined the naval officer on the quarter-deck.

Sullivan looked at them curiously. 'What's been going on?' he asked. 'We got the call signal, and your position, but that was all,' he declared. 'Since then we haven't been able to get a word out of you, so we concluded you were down somewhere, either in the sea or on one of the islands.'

'We were,' Biggles told him. 'Not that it would have made much difference if we'd been in the air.'

'Why not?'

'Because our wireless equipment is a nasty-looking heap of bits and pieces.'

Sullivan stared. 'How did you manage that?' he asked.

'*We* didn't manage it,' answered Biggles grimly. 'It was managed for us by a packet of bullets fired by a dirty skunk in a seaplane. Listen, and I'll tell you what happened, although we've no time to spare: there are several things we shall have to do before we leave, and I have a feeling that we're by no means safe here. We are close to the enemy stronghold, or my calculations are all at sea.' Briefly, he described how they had found the flying boat and its dead crew and how, while calling up the destroyer for assistance, they themselves had been shot down.

'It looks as if things are getting warm,' muttered Sullivan when he had finished.

'Warmish,' agreed Biggles, 'but they'll be warmer still presently, I fancy.'

'What's your programme; have you made one?'

'More or less. First of all, I want you to send a party ashore to bury poor Tom Lowery and his gunner. Get a report from the petty officer in charge to accompany mine to headquarters. He will find their personal effects lying near the crash where I dropped them when the *Nemesis* was attacked. They will be needed for the Court of Adjustment which I expect will be held at Singapore. While that's going on I want a couple of strong fellows, with cutlasses or billhooks, to help me find the seaplane. We may discover something important either in the machine or on the body of the pilot—maps—log-books—orders—you never know. As soon as we've done that you'd better push off back to the mainland out of harm's way while we get on with the job of finding the base. We shan't have far to look, if I know anything about it. It's going to be a bit awkward without wireless, but we shall have to manage without it for the time being.'

Biggles turned to Ginger. 'While I'm ashore, if Algy goes with the party to Tom's crash, as I hope he will, I shall leave you in charge of the machine. If by any chance you are attacked by another aircraft, run her up on to the beach and try to keep the fellow off with your gun until I get back. Don't attempt to take off. It's no use taking on a single-seater while you're by yourself in a machine of this size. Is that clear?'

'Quite, sir,' replied Ginger smartly, conscious of his responsibility, and that several pairs of curious eyes were on him.

A day of activity followed. It began with the destroyer's boat taking two parties ashore. The first consisted of Algy with a dozen bluejackets* equipped with picks and shovels, to whom had been allotted the dismal task of burying the two dead British airmen and collecting their effects. The second was smaller, being composed only of Biggles and two sailors who were to

*Slang: sailors.

help him to cut a way through the dense jungle to the hill-side on which the enemy seaplane had fallen.

Ginger spent rather a lonely day, but he utilized the time by going over the *Nemesis* very carefully, examining the controls and other parts where the hard wear to which the machine had been subjected might be beginning to show. Later, in the afternoon, he refuelled from the *Seafret*'s store, a task he was just completing when a sharp gust of wind caused the *Nemesis* to yaw violently and send his eyes skyward. What he saw brought a slight frown to his forehead, and he finished his task hurriedly; but before he could return to the *Seafret* a hail made him look up, and he saw Lovell, the Navigating Officer, looking over the rail.

'What do you make of this breeze?' he asked with a hint of anxiety in his voice.

'That's what I've come to tell you,' replied the naval officer. 'The barometer's falling; not much, but it looks as if we might be in for some weather. The skipper says it's the tail end of a big blow centred somewhere near the Philippines, but for an hour or two it's likely to get worse instead of better. What are you going to do?'

Ginger thought sharply. 'I think I'd better run the *Nemesis* up on the beach,' he answered. 'She'll be safe enough there. If I stay here and a sea gets up she may smash her wing-tips to splinters against your side. No, I'll get her ashore. Biggles can't be much longer, anyway, and if he'd rather she rode it out on the water he can tell me to bring her back when he comes down to the beach.'

'Hadn't you better take a man with you in case you need help?' suggested Lovell.

'Thanks! I think that's a sound idea,' agreed Ginger. 'If the wind freshens I may have to peg her down.'

'All right. Stand by, I'll send you a hand.'

With a parting wave the naval officer disappeared and a few moments later one of the bluejackets who had been helping with the refuelling, a lad named Gilmore, ran down the steps and joined Ginger in the cockpit. It was the work of a moment to cast off, start the engines, and turn the nose of the amphibian towards the sandy beach that fringed the bay. As they reached it, Ginger lowered the undercarriage wheels, and the aircraft crawled ashore like a great white seal.

'That's OK—she'll do here,' declared Ginger, as he turned her nose into the slight breeze and cut the engines. 'I believe we've had our trouble for nothing, after all; the wind seems to be dropping already.'

'I expect we shall get it in gusts for an hour or two,' replied the bluejacket professionally. 'Are you going to tie her up or anything?'

'Not yet. There isn't enough wind to hurt at the moment, so I think I'll wait for my skipper to come back and leave the decision to him. You can take a stroll round if you like, but keep within hail. I had a bad night so I'm a bit tired, and I think I shall stay here and rest.'

'Then if it's all the same to you I'll have a stroll outside,' decided the sailor. 'We don't often get a chance of putting our feet on dry land.'

'That suits me,' agreed Ginger, preparing to make himself comfortable, while the other jumped to the ground and disappeared under the wing.

A few minutes later Algy and his party, looking rather tired and depressed, emerged from the bushes, and while he was waiting for a boat to take him to the destroyer he expressed surprise at finding the *Nemesis* on the beach; but he nodded agreement when Ginger told him the reason.

'I think you're right,' he opined, as the destroyer's boat grated on the sand. 'You'd better wait here until Biggles comes back; he can't be very much longer.'

'Right-ho! See you presently, then,' nodded Ginger, returning to the cabin as Algy departed.

For what seemed to be a long time he sat in the machine with his feet up on the opposite seat, contemplating the project on which they were engaged; then, happening to glance at the sky through the window, he saw that its colour had turned to that soft shade of egg-shell blue that often precedes twilight. It struck him suddenly that it was getting late and, wondering what could be delaying Biggles, he rose to his feet, yawning, and looked out through the opposite window, which overlooked the jungle, casually and without any particular interest. But as he gazed a curious expression, in which incredulity, doubt, and alarm were all represented, stole over his face. He did not even finish his yawn, but allowed his lips to remain parted, while his eyes, from being half closed, slowly grew round with the intensity of their stare. The point on which they were focused was a narrow open space, not more than a couple of feet wide, between two clumps of fern-palm on the very edge of the jungle. It was already in deep shadow, but from out of its centre peeped a face, flat, wizened, surmounted by a tightly fitting skull-cap. It was perfectly still, so still that it might have been a mask. The eyes did not even blink, but remained fixed so steadfastly on the aircraft that Ginger, still staring at it, with his pulses tingling, began to wonder if it was real, or whether his imagination was playing tricks with him. Shaking himself impatiently, he rubbed his eyes and looked again. The face was no longer there.

The shock of this second discovery moved him to

action. Knowing how deceptive the half-light can be, he was still in doubt whether he had really seen what he thought he had seen. For a moment or two his eyes probed the edge of the jungle, scrutinizing every gap and clearing, but he could see no sign of life. He noticed that the wind had dropped, for everything was still, and the heavy silence that hung over the scene seemed to charge the atmosphere with a sinister influence. Then he noticed something else, or rather the absence of something. There were no monkeys on the beach, as there usually were on all the beaches of the island, seeking their evening meal of crabs and shellfish. Why? He remembered Gilmore. Where was he? What was he doing? Swiftly he made his way through to the cockpit and, without exposing himself, peeped over the edge.

The first thing he saw was Gilmore, lying on the soft sand under the wing, asleep. He seemed curiously still, ominously still, even for sleep. His position was an unusual one, too—more that of a person arrested in the act of stretching than sleeping, for his back was arched in an unnatural manner. Ginger could not see his face, but as he stared at him he felt a sudden unaccountable twinge of fear and shivered as if a draught of cold air had enveloped him.

'Gilmore,' he whispered.

The sailor did not move.

'Gilmore,' he said more loudly, a tremor creeping into his voice.

Still the man did not move.

Ginger moistened his lips, and lifted his eyes again to the edge of the jungle.

This time there was no mistake. For a fleeting instant he caught sight of a leering face. Then it was gone. But he distinctly saw it go, merge into the dark background rather than turn aside. His heart gave a lurch, and while he hesitated, uncertain for the moment how to act, he heard a soft *phut*, as if a light blow had fallen on the fuselage just below him.

Even in that moment of panic his first thought was of Biggles, out there in the shadowy jungle. A swift glance over his shoulder showed the *Seafret*, motionless at anchor. It seemed a long way away. Turning, he was just in time to see a vague shadow flit across a narrow clearing.

He waited no longer. Drawing his automatic, he took aim at the bush behind which the shadow had disappeared and fired. He saw another bush quiver, and he blazed at it recklessly, emptying his weapon except for a single round which he saved for emergency.

As the echoes of the shooting died away everything seemed to come to life at once. Scores of birds rose into the air with shrill cries of alarm. There was a chorus of shouts and sudden orders from the direction of the destroyer, while at the same time there was a loud crashing in the bushes not far from the beach.

Ginger, wondering if he had done the right thing, saw with relief that a boat had been lowered from the ship and was already racing towards the amphibian; but before it reached the shore Biggles, gun in hand, followed by his two men, had burst through the bushes looking swiftly to right and left for the cause of the uproar. He started when he saw the *Nemesis* high and dry on the beach, and broke into a run towards it, only to slow down again with questioning eyes as Ginger jumped out.

'What on earth's all the noise about?' he asked sharply, almost angrily.

Ginger, who had not yet recovered from his fright, pointed at the jungle. 'Be careful,' he shouted, almost hysterically. 'Watch out—they're in there.'

'Who's in there? What's in there?'

'Savages! Something—I don't know,' answered Ginger incoherently.

The destroyer's boat reached the beach and, without waiting for it to be pulled up, Algy and several sailors armed with rifles leapt ashore and raced up to where the others were standing.

'What's going on?' asked Algy quickly, looking from one to the other in turn.

'I'm dashed if I know,' replied Biggles. 'Come on, Ginger, pull yourself together. What did you see?'

'Faces, in the bushes.'

'You haven't been dreaming, have you?'

Before Ginger could answer, a cry of horror broke from the lips of one of the sailors and, swinging round, the others saw him staring ashen-faced at Gilmore, still lying in the dark shadow under the wing. Ginger took one look at the bared teeth and staring eyes, and then covered his face with his hands.

Biggles shook him roughly. 'How did it happen?' he snapped.

But a Chief Petty Officer who had seen much service in the Far East had taken in the situation at a glance.

'Cover those bushes,' he cried tersely to the sailors who were armed, 'and shoot at anything you see move.' He turned to Biggles. 'It looks like Malay work to me, sir,' he said crisply. 'We don't want to lose any more men if we can help it. It's no use trying to fight them on their own ground, so we'd better retreat. Gilmore was killed by a blow-pipe—look at this.' He held up a tiny pointed dart, discoloured at the tip. 'One scratch of that and you're a goner inside ten minutes,' he declared. 'I've seen 'em before.'

'Where did you find that?' asked Biggles quickly.

'Stuck in the nose of your aeroplane.'

'Were you attacked, Ginger?' inquired Biggles.

'No. I only thought I saw a face, but it put the wind up me and, knowing you were still in the jungle, I fell into a panic, thinking perhaps a crowd of them were lying in wait for you.'

'I should say they would have had you, sir, if they'd known you were in there,' the Chief Petty Officer told Biggles seriously. 'They've cleared off now by the look of it, but they won't have gone far away. We don't want to be caught here in the dark, so I suggest that you give orders for every one to return to the boat; and I'd take the aeroplane out, too, sir, or you won't find much of it left in the morning.'

'What made you bring her ashore?' Biggles asked Ginger as they started the engines.

'A breeze got up, and I was told that the glass was falling, so I thought she'd be safer ashore than on the water.'

'Yes, you were right there,' admitted Biggles, as he eased the throttle forward and ran down into the sea. 'It's a bad business about that sailor being killed,' he went on moodily. 'Sullivan will jolly soon be getting fed up with me. I don't know what's wrong, but nothing seems to be going right on this trip. We've had nothing but casualties since the time we started.'

'Well, it's no use getting depressed about it,' put in Algy. 'Let's get aboard and call a council of war.'

'I think that's the best thing we can do,' agreed Biggles despondently. 'It's getting time we did something. So far the enemy seem to have had things pretty well their own way.'

Chapter 9
A Nasty Customer

Sullivan awaited them with a gloomy face when, with the island a silent world of indigo shadows behind them, they returned to the destroyer, for the body of the dead sailor had preceded them. He did not speak, but his eyes rested on Biggles face questioningly.

'Let's go below,' suggested Biggles curtly.

In single file they made their way to the commander's cabin, where the three airmen threw off their coats and sank wearily into such seats as they could find, for although the port-hole was wide open, the atmosphere was heavy and oppressive.

'I'm afraid you're beginning to feel that I am making a mess of this business,' began Biggles, looking at the naval officer, who had seated himself at his desk, and, with his chin cupped in his left hand, was moodily drawing invisible lines on the blotting-pad, with the end of a ruler.

Sullivan glanced up. 'No,' he said. 'One can't make an omelette without breaking eggs, and one can't conduct a war without casualties; but I must admit that I'm beginning to wonder if we haven't taken on something rather beyond our limited resources.'

'I'm beginning to wonder the same thing,' confessed Biggles slowly, biting his lower lip and staring morosely through the open port-hole to where the distant, gentle swell of the sea was beginning to turn from navy blue to black. 'It's these casualties that depress me,' he went on. 'I'm not used to them. In the past we've taken many risks, willingly, even as we are prepared to take them now, but this losing of men—' He broke off and began walking slowly up and down the cabin. 'All the same, I don't think we can stop now whatever the cost may be,' he continued bitterly. 'I suppose you know as much as we do about what happened on the beach just now?'

'The Chief Petty Officer in charge of the shore party gave me a verbal report.'

'Where have these people come from suddenly? They weren't here yesterday, I'll swear.'

'Why are you so sure of that?'

'Because if they had been they would have molested us. Had they been here they would certainly have seen us land, and, scattered as we were, it would have been the easiest thing in the world to have bumped us off. Moreover, they would have been to Tom Lowery's crash, if only to look for plunder, yet nothing had been touched. I tell you, Sullivan, these people—whoever they are—came here to-day. Have you seen any native craft about?'

'I haven't seen a craft of any sort for days except a junk, beating north, well out to sea.'

'A junk! When did you see a junk?'

'This morning.'

'Was it under steam or sail?'

'Both, I fancy, judging by the speed she was moving, although she was too far away for me to say with certainty.'

'What sail was she carrying?'

'A mains'l and a jib—or what goes for them.'

'Was the mains'l red and the jib yellow, by any chance?'

Sullivan raised his eyebrows. 'Why, yes, that's right,' he answered quickly.

Biggles thrust his hands deep into his pockets, and, coming to a standstill, faced the commander squarely. 'I saw that same craft—let me see, when would it be?—yesterday morning. But it was a long way north of here. I don't understand—' He wrinkled his forehead as he pondered the problem. 'What course was this junk on when you saw her?' he asked.

'Mainly north, but I wouldn't swear that she wasn't making a little westerly.'

'Westerly, eh! That means that even if you had watched her you would have lost sight of her as she passed behind the next island—what's the name of it?'

'Lattimer Island.'

'That's right.'

'What are you trying to get at?'

'I'm trying to work out how a boat could have landed these toughs on the island since we came here without our knowing it. Mind you, even if that is what happened it doesn't necessarily follow that they are connected with the people we are up against.'

'Is it possible that they could have landed?'

'Certainly—if the junk beat back to the far side of the island after disappearing behind Lattimer Island.'

'Then you think the junk's still hanging about not far away?'

'I shouldn't be surprised.'

'Well, we can soon satisfy ourselves on that point,' declared Sullivan. 'Let's have the anchor up and sail round the island. How does that strike you?'

Algy noticed that Biggles was staring at Sullivan with a most extraordinary expression on his face; heard him say 'No' in a detached sort of way, as if he were suddenly disinterested in the conversation. Then he appeared to recover himself.

'No, I don't think there's any necessity for that,' he

exclaimed, in a firm voice. 'To tell you the truth, I'm half inclined to think that Ginger's imagination got away with him when he was ashore, and that Gilmore died from snake-bite.'

Ginger stared at Biggles incredulously, wondering what had suddenly come over him. His manner was most odd. Without looking at them, he had walked the length of the cabin, turned at right-angles, and, with his eyes on the floor, was now walking back as close to the wall as possible. Near to the port-hole he stopped, facing them, as if grateful for the slight change of temperature the position afforded.

'What I hope most of all,' he continued, 'is that my staff have not lost their capacity for prompt action.' He spoke quietly, but there was a curious inflection in his voice, and Ginger quivered suddenly as the full significance of the words dawned on him. Something was about to happen. But what?

'I don't understand you,' muttered Sullivan, frowning. 'What on earth are you talking about?'

'I'll show you,' answered Biggles, and whirling round, he thrust his right hand and arm far through the port-hole.

The others heard him catch his breath, saw him take a quick pace backwards, bracing himself as if to support a weight, at the same time jerking his arm inwards. They all sprang to their feet as a brown face, wearing an expression of astonished alarm, appeared in the circular brass frame of the port-hole. Biggles's fingers were twisted in the long hair.

'Outside, Sullivan,' he snapped. 'You'll have to get him from the outside. Jump to it! Algy, get your hands round his neck—I daren't let go his hair. It's all right, he can't get his arms through.'

The whole thing had happened in an instant of time,

but after the first speechless second the spectators moved swiftly. Sullivan darted through the doorway. There was a rush of feet on deck. Algy, as he had been bidden, took the eavesdropper's neck in his hands in a grip that threatened to choke him.

'Go steady,' said Biggles tersely. 'Don't throttle him. I shall want him to be able to talk presently.'

It was an extraordinary situation. The man, now snarling with rage, had his head through the port-hole and his shoulders jammed tightly against the frame, the rest of his body being outside. Clearly, the capture would have to be effected from without, for the port-hole was much too small for the man's body to go through it.

There came a splash of a boat on the water, and muffled words outside.

'All right, sir, let go; we've got him,' said some one.

Biggles and Algy released their grips. The face disappeared, and a moment later Sullivan walked back into the cabin, smiling.

'By gosh! That was smart work,' he exclaimed. 'How the dickens did you know he was there?'

'I saw his fingers as he pulled himself up,' answered Biggles. 'Or rather, I saw the reflection of his fingers in that mirror.' He pointed to a small square mirror on the opposite wall. 'They only appeared for a moment,' he went on, 'because once the fellow was up he could keep his balance in the canoe, or whatever he was in, by just resting his hands on the outside of the destroyer. He was in a very nice place, too, because not only could he hear every word we said, but he could see us—or our reflections—in the mirror, without our seeing him. That's what made it so awkward. I daren't warn you by word or action for fear he bolted. That is why I didn't agree with you about making a search for the junk. I had just seen him, and I was afraid he'd be off to tell his pals what was afoot before I could collar him. I daren't leave the room either, in case he took it as a sign that he had been spotted; all I could do was make a grab in the dark and hope for the best. Luckily I managed to get him by the hair. What was he in—a boat?'

'Not he. A boat would have been seen by the watch, as he knew jolly well. He was standing on a length of tree-trunk; paddled himself here beside it with only his nose out of the water, I expect. No doubt he saw the light in the port-hole and made it his objective, which, as it turned out, was a pretty shrewd choice. What about this junk though?'

'Let's hear what the prisoner has to say for himself before we make any decision about that.'

'I doubt if he can speak English.'

'I should say he can, otherwise he wouldn't have been sent here. I mean to say, he was probably selected for the job on account of that qualification.'

There was a murmur outside the door, and a knock; it was then thrown open to admit four men: the Chief Petty Officer who had been in charge of the shore-party and two sailors who between them held the prisoner by the arms, although his wrists had been handcuffed behind his back. He was stark naked and dripping wet. Lank black hair hung half-way down his neck.

'Will you do the questioning?' invited Sullivan, looking at Biggles.

Biggles nodded. 'I'll ask him a few things first, and then, if there's anything else you want to know, you can have a go.' He sat down and fixed his eyes on the man's face.

'What's your nationality?' he asked, speaking very distinctly.

The man glowered and made no reply.

'Come on, you can speak English.'

Not by a single sign did the prisoner betray that he understood.

A hard glint came into Biggles's eyes. 'You heard me,' he rapped out sharply. 'Where have you come from?'

The man only stared at him sullenly.

Biggles nodded grimly. 'I see; it's like that, is it?' he said slowly. 'Listen here, my man. You're on a British warship, and if you behave yourself you'll have a fair trial, but if you try being awkward you'll find that we can be awkward, too. Now then. Who sent you to this ship?'

Still the prisoner did not answer.

Biggles glanced at Sullivan. 'Do you think your stokers could loosen his tongue?' he asked meaningly.

The commander nodded. 'Yes,' he said simply, 'they'd make a dumb man speak if I told them to.'

'Very well. Let them take him below and see what they can do,' ordered Biggles harshly. 'And you can tell them if they fail they needn't bring him back here; tell them to open one of the furnaces and throw him in.' Biggles eyelids flickered slightly as he caught Ginger's gaze on him.

The prisoner stirred uneasily, and his little eyes flashed from one to the other of his interrogators.

'All right! Take him away,' said Biggles shortly,

'No! I speak,' gasped the prisoner desperately.

'You'd be well advised to do so,' Biggles told him grimly. 'My patience is at an end. What is your nationality.'

'No understand—nashnalty.'

'Where do you come from?'

'Me stay Singapore.'

'Where did you come from before that?'
'Manila.'
'I see. Who is your master.'
'He no name.'
'Where is he?'
The man hesitated.
'Come on!'
'He on junk.'
'Where is the junk?'
The prisoner's eyes switched nervously to the porthole, as if he feared he might be overheard. 'Junk he lay offside island—round headland,' he whispered hoarsely.
Biggles half smiled at Sullivan at this piece of vital information. Then he looked back at the prisoner, who, he suspected, was a Malay Dyak with Chinese or Japanese blood in his veins. 'What is the junk doing in this sea?' he asked crisply.
The man screwed up his face. 'Not know,' he answered earnestly.
Biggles thought he was telling the truth and turned again to Sullivan. 'I don't think there's much point in prolonging this interview,' he said. 'Have you any questions for him?'
'No.'
'All right. Take him away. Keep him in irons and under guard,' Biggles told the Chief Petty Officer.
'I don't think we shall get any more information out of him,' he continued, as the prisoner was marched out, 'for the simple reason that he doesn't know what it's all about. I fancy he is just a deckhand sent over to listen because he knows a smattering of English. We shall do more good by having a closer look at this junk.'

'Absolutely,' agreed the naval officer promptly. 'Shall we move off right away?'

Biggles pondered for a moment. 'No, I don't think so,' he said. 'If they hear us or see the ship moving they'll know what we're after and perhaps give us the slip. If it's agreeable to you I'd rather put an armed party in the long-boat and try and take the junk that way. We should be able to creep along close to the shore—closer than you dare risk in the destroyer. In fact, we might get right up to the junk without being spotted.'

'I think perhaps you're right,' agreed Sullivan. 'How many men will you need?'

'A score should be enough. Serve them out with cutlasses and pistols.'

'Good enough. When will you start?'

'Just as soon as you can detail a party and put the boat on the water.'

Sullivan moved towards the door. 'Five minutes will be enough for that,' he promised.

His time estimate was not far out, for inside ten minutes the boat was on the water creeping stealthily towards the shore. Biggles sat in the stern with Lovell, for Sullivan could not, of course, leave his ship. Ginger, who with some difficulty had persuaded Biggles to allow him to accompany the party, sat just in front. Following the policy of always leaving a pilot with the *Nemesis*, Algy, much to his disgust, had been left behind.

The air was still. In the pale light of a crescent moon the silhouette of the island was very beautiful, and as they crept along the deserted shore, occasionally catching the perfume of the flowering shrubs that backed the white sandy beach, Ginger was enchanted with the peace and loveliness of the whole setting, and more than half regretted the business on which they were engaged. He would have much preferred to play at Robinson Crusoe for a little while, for there were many things of interest, both in the water, where brightly coloured fish swam unafraid amongst pink and yellow coral, and on the shore, where everything that lived was new to him.

The sailors rowed without speaking, for conversation had been forbidden, and in the fairy-like surroundings a curious feeling crept over Ginger that he was dreaming. But when, presently, rounding a headland, the bare masts and ungainly hulk of a junk came into view against the deep purple sky, a thrill ran through him, and he sensed the tension of the moment in the quick intaking of breath of the men in front of him.

'Easy all,' said Biggles softly, and then, as the sailors rested their oars, he continued: 'Take it quietly every one until I give the word, then put your backs into it. The boarding party will avoid bloodshed if possible. I hope the enemy will surrender, but if we meet with resistance, which we may take as proof of guilt, then use your weapons. Bo'sun, you know more about these things than I do. Select two good men, and the instant you get aboard make for the captain's quarters. It is important that he should not have a chance of destroying anything. That's all. Now then, gently does it.'

As the boat moved forward over the smooth surface of the water, leaving only a phosphorescent ripple to mark her passage, Biggles leaned forward and spoke to Ginger. 'You keep close to me,' he said severely. 'There's no sense in you getting your head sliced off by a crazy Dyak armed with half a yard of razor-edged steel. The sailors will attend to the fighting, if there is any.'

They were not more than a hundred yards from the

junk when a shrill cry warned them that they had been seen.

'All right, my lads, let her go,' roared Biggles, abandoning all attempt at concealment. 'Junk ahoy!'

There was another shout. A firearm flashed and the missile richocheted off the water not far away. The deep breathing of the sailors told of the efforts they were making, and within a few seconds of the alarm the boat had run alongside the larger vessel. There was a mighty swirl as the oars backed water, and then what seemed to Ginger a moment's confusion as the boarding party jumped to their feet and swarmed over the side, Biggles amongst them. There was a blinding flash and a deafening roar as a firearm exploded at point-blank range, and a sailor fell back into the boat, swearing fluently and clutching his shoulder. Simultaneously a clamour broke out above, exaggerated in its volume by the preceding silence—shouts and screams punctuated by thuds and occasionally shots.

Ginger could stand it no longer. Grabbing at the loose end of a trailing rope, he went up the side of the junk like a monkey and threw his leg over the rail. All he could see at first was a confused mêlée of running men, but presently he was able to make out that there was a certain amount of order about it, and that the sailors were driving the crew of the junk before them into the bows. One or two of the orientals had climbed into the rigging, and he saw another deliberately dive overboard. The men in the rigging rather worried him; he wondered if the sailors had overlooked them, and with his automatic in his hand he had stepped forward to warn them when he saw Biggles leave the party and hurry towards the companion-way, evidently with the idea of following the bo'sun below, assuming that he had carried out his orders and rushed for the captain's quarters.

Ginger saw that Biggles would have to pass immediately below the men in the rigging, so he shouted a warning. 'Watch out, Biggles—up above you!' he yelled, and to emphasize his words he threw up his pistol and fired without taking any particular aim. He did not hit any of the men aloft—not that he expected to—but the shot may have saved Biggles, for with a crisp thud a knife buried itself in the planking near his feet.

He leapt aside, calling to the sailors as he did so. Two or three of them broke away from the party in the bows, and pointing their weapons upwards, induced the natives to come down. It marked the end of the resistance, which had only been half-hearted at the best, and Ginger, following Biggles below, was just in time to witness the last act of a tragedy.

In the corner of a large, well-furnished room, evidently the captain's cabin, stood a modern steel safe with its door wide open. Below it, on the ground, lay a number of papers. Near by stood a small, dark-skinned man in blue uniform, covered by the revolvers of the two sailors who had been detailed by the bo'sun to accompany him. Such was the position as Biggles strode through the doorway with Ginger at his heels. But at that moment there was a muffled report. The dark-skinned man swayed for a moment, and then pitched forward on to his face.

The bo'sun, who had been kneeling near the safe collecting the papers, sprang to his feet. 'Who did that?' he cried.

'The fool shot himself,' answered one of the sailors.

The bo'sun looked at Biggles and shrugged his

shoulders. 'I didn't think of him doing that, sir,' he explained apologetically.

'Couldn't be helped,' Biggles told him quietly. 'Pick up those papers will you, and collect anything that is left in the safe. Make a thorough search of the room and bring me any other papers you find. I shall be on deck.' Then, turning, he saw Ginger. 'What are you doing here?' he asked. 'I told you to keep out of the way. Still, it doesn't matter now; it's all over by the look of it. Let's get up on deck.'

At the head of the companion-way they met Lovell, who seemed to be labouring under a high degree of excitement. 'I was just coming to fetch you,' he exclaimed. 'Come and take a look at this.'

The others followed him quickly to where a hatch, with its cover thrown aside, lay like a square of black linoleum on the deck.

'Cast your eyes down there,' he invited them with a peculiar expression on his face, as a torch flashed in his hand, the beam probing the depths of the hold.

Biggles looked, and Ginger, taking a pace forward, looked too. At first he could not make out what it was upon which the yellow rays of the torch flashed so brightly; there seemed to be four long steel tubes, about a foot in diameter. His eyes followed them along to the end, and he saw that each terminated in a point.

'Torpedoes,' said Biggles, in a funny sort of whisper.

'Yes, they're "mouldies" all right,' grinned Lovell. 'There are also some cases of small-arms ammunition in the forward hold, and some shells, large ones and small ones that look like anti-aircraft tackle.'

Biggles glanced up to where the crew of the junk were huddled in the bows under the watchful eyes of the sailors. 'I think we had better get those beauties below and batten them down,' he suggested. 'You remain here with your fellows while I go back and have a word with Sullivan about this.'

Twenty minutes later he was telling the commander of the destroyer the result of the raid and what had been found on the junk. The documents from the safe, still unexamined, lay on the table.

When he had finished Sullivan rubbed his chin reflectively. His face was grave. 'We're sailing in tricky waters, Bigglesworth, and no mistake,' he said anxiously. 'Goodness knows what might not happen if we make a blunder. I don't want to go down to posterity as the man who plunged the world into a war of destruction, and it might be as bad as that if we slip up. But there, you're in charge. It's up to you to decide on a course of action, and to that I have only one thing to add. You can rely on me to stand by you to the bitter end.'

'Thanks, Sullivan,' answered Biggles simply. 'I know how you feel about the frightful responsibility of this thing. In the ordinary way a matter as serious as this would be reported to the Admiralty and probably to the Cabinet. It's their pigeon really, but we simply haven't time to work through those channels. Finding those "mouldies" tells us what we want to know. These enemy operations are no myth. They're a fact, and we're within a few miles of the headquarters of the organization. I said I'd find it and blot it out, and those are the lines on which I'm going to proceed regardless of what the result may be. But first of all we've got to dispose of this junk and its crew. Obviously we can't let them go loose or the fat would be in the fire before we could say Jack Robinson. Frankly, as far as I can see there's only one thing we can do with them.'

'What's that?'

'Set them ashore here on this island. Maroon them. Without a boat they wouldn't be able to leave until some one picked them up, by which time we should either have finished the job or be where it wouldn't matter much whether it was finished or not.'

'And the junk?'

'Bring one of the torpedoes aboard the *Seafret* for evidence in case it is ever needed, and then scuttle her.'

Sullivan nodded. 'Yes, I think that's the best way,' he agreed.

'Then you'd better send a message to Lovell to ask him to bring the junk along. It's easier to do that than for us to go round to her because it means moving the aircraft as well. Now let's see what we've got here.' He turned to the papers still lying on the table, and gave an exclamation of disgust when he saw that they were all penned in Oriental characters.

'Any of your fellows able to read this stuff?' he asked Sullivan.

The naval officer shook his head. 'No,' he said. 'That's an expert's job, and a sailor who could do it wouldn't be serving in a destroyer.'

'Pity. You'd better put them in your safe, then, for the time being. I wonder if this will tell us anything.' He picked up a chart that the Chief Petty Officer had brought over with the other papers. 'Aha! Aha! What's this?' he went on quickly, pointing to a number of fine pencil lines that converged on a point amid a group of islands that he recognized instantly as part of the Mergui Archipelago. Indeed, he had looked at the same section of the globe so often of late that he could have drawn a chart from memory. He looked at Sullivan with eyes that held a sparkle of triumph. 'So it's Elephant Island,' he said quietly.

'Looks like it,' agreed the other. 'That's all we want to know, isn't it?'

'It *would* be, if we were quite sure,' answered Biggles cautiously. 'Unfortunately we daren't take anything for granted in this affair. After all, for all we know, this point—' he laid his forefinger on the chart—'might merely be a sub-depot at which the skipper of the junk had been ordered to deliver his goods. We mustn't overlook that.'

'By jingo, yes. I'm afraid I had overlooked that possibility,' confessed Sullivan, 'That means—'

'It means that before we dare strike we've got to confirm that Elephant Island is, in fact, the base we are looking for.'

'How do you propose to do that?'

'I don't know,' answered Biggles frankly. 'I shall have to think about it. How far are we away from the place—forty miles?'

'Nearer thirty, I should say at a rough guess.'

'That's plenty close enough to be healthy,' declared Biggles. 'I'll think things over for a little while. Perhaps it would be better to sleep on it and have another conference in the morning. Meanwhile, let's get this business of the junk settled.'

'Right you are,' agreed Sullivan. 'Just a minute, though,' he went on quickly, as Biggles turned away. 'There's something I've been wanting to ask you, but what with one thing and another I haven't had a chance. What about that seaplane? Did you find anything of importance?'

Biggles nodded. 'I know who made the aircraft,' he said softly, giving the naval officer a queer look. He leaned forward and whispered something in his ear.

'Was there nothing on the pilot?' asked Sullivan.

'There wasn't any pilot,' replied Biggles grimly. 'The crocs—or a panther—got to him first.'

Chapter 10
A Risky Plan

The pink of dawn was fast turning to azure the following morning as, watched by the three airmen and the entire ship's company, the junk sank slowly out of sight beneath the limpid blue waters of the bay, carrying with her the body of her dead captain, which had seemed the most befitting burial they could give him.

As the mainmast disappeared from view Biggles turned his eyes towards the island on which the crew had been put ashore, but not a soul was in sight. 'You gave them plenty of stores, I suppose?' he asked, looking at Sullivan.

'Ample,' was the brief reply.

'Good! Then that's that,' observed Biggles, turning away from the rail.

'Have you decided what you are going to do?' inquired the naval officer.

Biggles nodded. 'Yes,' he said, 'but to tell you the truth, I am not absolutely convinced that it is the right thing. It's rather a tricky problem, whichever way you look at it. As I see it, there are two courses open to us in this matter of getting confirmation that Elephant Island is the place we're looking for. I think you'll agree that we must do that before taking any action. I mean, it would be a dickens of a mess if we went and blew up a friendly village, or a bunch of innocent Salones, wouldn't it?'

'It certainly would,' agreed Sullivan.

'Very well, then. We're agreed that we've got to have

a look at this place. There are two ways in which we can do it. One is to fly over it, and the other is to tackle it from ground level. At first glance the flying method might strike you as being far and away the easier, the same as it did me; but is it? If our friends know we're about, and I have an inkling that they do, they'll be watching the sky, that's certain. At the worst they might shoot us down, for while I am not without experience in the business of air combat, I don't feel in the least inclined to take on a bunch of single-seater fighters—or even one, if it comes to that—in an amphibian which, while it may be a good ship for our job, was never designed for fast combat work. Even one fast interceptor, flown by a determined pilot, could make things thundering uncomfortable for us; I've no delusions about that. Even if they didn't succeed in shooting us down they would know from the very fact that we were flying over their hide-out that we had spotted it, in which case they would either abandon the place forthwith and start again somewhere else, or else clean things up to such an extent that we should have no apparent justification for tackling them. You see what I mean?'

The others nodded.

'On the other hand,' continued Biggles, 'if, by scouting on foot, I could prove beyond all possible doubt that Elephant Island is the nest from which our ships have been sunk, the immediate result would be quite different. They would not know they had been spotted, and we should catch them red-handed, as it were. If their suspicions *have* been aroused they'll be far less likely to expect us to land on the island than choose the more obvious course of flying over it, or sailing round it in a ship.'

'I'm not anxious to sail my ship round it,' declared Sullivan emphatically.

'You'd be a fool if you did, and deserve what you'd probably get,' Biggles assured him. 'That's why I vote for the "on foot" method, although, coming from a pilot, that may strike you as odd. In my experience, though, the unorthodox, the unexpected, is always preferable to the obvious.'

'It seems to be asking for trouble, to land on the very island that the enemy have made their perishing headquarters,' murmured Algy doubtfully.

'I suppose it is,' agreed Biggles, 'but then so is anything else that we could do. And, anyway, we expected that we should have to take risks when we started, didn't we? In fact, whenever a job has been offered us that involved no risk, you've usually been the first to turn your nose up. But we're wasting time. I'm going to Elephant Island.'

'What, alone?'

'No, I'm taking Ginger with me.'

'And what about me?' asked Algy.

'Oh, there'll be a job for you, don't you worry,' Biggles told him. 'Now listen; I've given a good deal of thought to this proposition and this is my idea. We lie low here until it gets dark, when, provided the weather remains fine, the *Seafret* will take us—that is, the *Nemesis*—in tow to Hastings Island. We shall then be a lot nearer to Elephant Island than we are here. According to Sailing Directions, which I have looked up, there is a lagoon with a good anchorage at the eastern end of Hastings Island that should suit us very well as a temporary base. It's rather close to the enemy, I know, and it would be out of the question for a prolonged stay, but I'm hoping that we shan't be there many hours. Anyway, it wouldn't do for the *Seafret* to drift about on the open sea, or the next thing will be a torpedo in *her* ribs.' Biggles glanced at Sullivan, who nodded agreement.

'I hadn't overlooked the possibility of that,' he observed drily.

'All right, then,' continued Biggles. 'Now somebody has got to stay with the *Nemesis*. That's definite. I'm going ashore, so it will have to be you, Algy. The next move will be made as soon as it gets dark, when the *Seafret* will steam slowly to within a mile or two of the south-east corner of Elephant Island, where she will lower a dinghy in which Ginger and I will row ashore. If you look at the chart you will notice that just off that particular piece of coast there are a number of small islets, bare rocks for the most part, I fancy. Some of them almost touch the main island. We—that is, Ginger and I—will make for those islets and find a good hiding-place. Having settled that, Ginger will then put me ashore, and afterwards return to the hiding-place, where he will lie doggo until he gets my signal to come and fetch me. You get the idea? We daren't risk leaving the boat on the actual beach of the main island in case any one happens to come along. By parking it behind one of the islets it will be out of sight. Naturally, the *Seafret* will return to Hastings Island as soon as she has dropped Ginger and me in the dinghy. So the position will be this. I shall be ashore, scouting. Ginger will be with the dinghy hiding behind the islet waiting to pick me up. You, Algy, will be at Hastings Island with the *Nemesis*, where the *Seafret* will rejoin you as soon as she can.'

'And after that?' asked Algy.

'As soon as I discover what I hope to discover,' went on Biggles, 'I shall return to the beach and whistle for Ginger to pick me up, whereupon we return to the hiding-place behind the islet and remain there all day. As soon as it gets dark, and, before the moon rises, the *Seafret* will come back and pick us both up.'

'But wait a minute,' cried Algy. 'I don't get the hang of this. Why not let the *Seafret* dump us all ashore and stand by until we've finished the job? It can then pick us up again and the whole thing will be over in one go.'

Biggles lit a cigarette. 'I expected you'd suggest that,' he murmured. 'Admittedly, at first glance there seems much to recommend that plan, but if you examine it closely you'll see that there are certain difficulties. In the first place, there is a time factor, and it is very important. The *Seafret* can only approach Elephant Island while there is no moon; it would be absolutely fatal for her to be within five miles of the place after that. You know what tropical moonlight is like as well as I do—we might as well go in daylight. Any one on the island would only have to look out to sea to spot her. I don't think I could possibly hope to explore the island and get back to the boat in sufficient time to enable the *Seafret* to get over the horizon before moonrise.'

'Why not let her hide amongst those islets you've spoken about?'

Biggles frowned. 'Be reasonable, my dear fellow,' he said. 'It would take more nerve than I've got to ask Sullivan to take his ship amongst a maze of strange rocks and reefs, many no doubt uncharted, in the pitch dark. The *Seafret* would probably rip her bottom off inside five minutes, and that would just about put the tin hat on everything. I've taken all that into account, and that's why I'm of opinion that the plan I have outlined is the best. Besides, Ginger and I in a little boat would make a very mobile unit, able to dodge about anywhere with very little risk of being seen.'

'Then there's nothing I can do?' asked Algy.

'I'm coming to that,' answered Biggles. 'Now if we—that is, Ginger and I—do our job, and the *Seafret* picks us up as per schedule, all so well and good. The *Nemesis* won't be needed for the moment. But suppose something goes wrong. Suppose I got delayed on the island for some reason or other. If the worst came to the worst you'd have to fly over and look for me. Naturally, if I was free to do so I should make for a place where you could get the machine down. I couldn't ask Sullivan to charge round the island looking for me, but at a pinch you could do that, although you'd be taking a tidy risk. It would be a case where you would have to use your initiative and act for the best, but I must say it would be a big consolation to me to know that if for any reason I couldn't get back to the boat, there was a second string to our fiddle in the shape of the *Nemesis*.'

'Yes, I see that,' admitted Algy; 'but I can't help feeling that there are a lot of loose joints in this scheme.'

'I know; that's why I'm not infatuated with it myself,' confessed Biggles. 'But it's the best plan I can think of. We've got to know what's happening on Elephant Island, and we've got to know pretty soon. It won't be long before the enemy will be wondering what has happened to the junk, which presumably was a supply ship, and while I don't think it's likely, there is always a risk of one of those men we put ashore getting down to Elephant Island and spilling the beans good and proper—as they say on the films.'

'But how could he do that?'

'They might make a raft, or a dug-out canoe.'

'Then why did you turn them loose?'

'What else could we do with them? Had I been a

hard-baked pirate I could have bumped the whole lot off, shot them, hung them, or sent them to Davy Jones in the hold of their junk; but wholesale murder isn't in our line, not even though we are virtually at war. There were too many of them to keep as prisoners on the *Seafret*.'

'Yes, I suppose you're right,' agreed Algy doubtfully. 'When is this programme due to start?'

'This evening, as soon as it's dark. As we're so close to the enemy's stronghold we should be crazy to start cruising about either on the water or in the air in broad daylight.'

'And suppose Elephant Island *is* the enemy stronghold, what then?' asked Ginger.

'Let's do one thing at a time,' suggested Biggles. 'It's always sound policy.'

Chapter 11
Horrors from the Deep

When Biggles and Ginger set out the following evening in accordance with the carefully considered plan of campaign, Biggles—although he did not say so—felt that the end of the affair might well be in sight, and he derived some relief from the thought, for both the importance of his task and the magnitude of his responsibilities weighed heavily upon him, and filled him with an unusual nervousness concerning the issue. The reason may have been that, whereas most of his adventures hitherto had been of a personal nature, the present one involved considerations so momentous that they appalled him. A single indiscretion might, he knew, embarrass the leaders of the Empire at a singularly inopportune time, and failure at the crucial moment would almost certainly precipitate a world war.

That was no doubt why he was inclined to be taciturn as he leaned over the *Seafret*'s rail watching the inky water glide past as the destroyer thrust her hatchet bows into the darkness in the direction of Elephant Island. Ginger, sensing his anxiety as he stood beside him, said nothing, but stared moodily at the bridge, on which the vague silhouette of Commander Sullivan's head and shoulders could just be seen against the sky. Algy, as arranged, had been left behind with the *Nemesis* at the Hastings Island anchorage.

'What's the time?' asked Biggles at last. 'We must be nearly there.'

Ginger looked at his wrist watch. 'Twenty to ten,' he answered quietly.

'Another five minutes,' murmured Biggles, obviously glad that the time for action was at hand, for the sepulchral gloom that surrounded the ship, which, of course, was showing no lights, did nothing to enliven the proceedings.

A minute or two later the barely perceptible vibration of the destroyer's engines ceased, and Sullivan joined them.

'Here we are,' he said. 'It's as black as pitch. I'm afraid you're going to find things rather difficult until the moon gets up.'

'You put a compass in the dinghy?'

'Yes, with a tin of food and a beaker of water.'

'That's all right, then. We shan't miss the island, although I shall have to wait for moonrise before I start operations.' Biggles turned and walked slowly towards the davits where a number of sailors were preparing to lower a small boat. 'I shall expect you back about the same time tomorrow night,' he told Sullivan quietly as he climbed into the suspended dinghy. 'If it's very dark I may have to whistle for you; we daren't risk showing lights. If you *do* see me show a light you'll know things are pretty urgent.'

'Good enough. Best of luck,' was the naval officer's farewell as the boat was lowered to the water.

Biggles picked up an oar and pushed the dinghy clear; then, after rowing for a short distance, he paused to make himself comfortable and arrange the compass on the seat in front of him.

Ginger, in the stern, could do nothing but sit still and watch him. When he next looked behind him the destroyer had merged into the black background of night. They were alone.

'We have some funny sort of picnics, don't we?' he murmured, for the sake of something to say, for the darkness, the silence, and the lap of water on the keel all combined to create an atmosphere of mystery that was by no means conducive to peace of mind.

'This hardly comes in the category of picnic, I think, and I shall be surprised if you haven't endorsed my opinion by the time the day dawns,' replied Biggles softly. 'Keep your eyes open and tell me if you see anything which looks like a rock or an island.'

For some time Biggles rowed in silence; then he looked up, resting on his oars. 'See anything?' he asked.

'I shouldn't be able to see a church if there was one an oar's length away,' declared Ginger. 'It's as black as your hat.'

'Then we'll take it easy until the moon wakes up and does its stuff,' said Biggles. 'We've only about another ten minutes to wait.'

He was quite right. In seven or eight minutes a faint luminosity in the sky provided enough light for them to see about them, and they were relieved to find that their position was as they intended it should be. Lying right across their bows lay the solid black mass of Elephant Island; nearer, not more than two hundred yards away, was the nearest of the rocky islets behind which they proposed to take cover. Several similar islets, all smaller, dotted the dark surface of the gently heaving waters.

Biggles dipped his oars again and the dinghy forged forward, leaving a gleaming trail of phosphorescence in her wake. The water that dripped from the blades of the oars each time they were raised flashed like molten silver, and Ginger watched it, fascinated; but he had no time to remark on it, for their objective was at hand, and reaching over the side he grabbed at a projecting piece of rock to steady the boat. There was no beach. The islet was just a mass of rock, roughly oval in shape, perhaps two hundred yards long and forty or fifty feet wide at the widest part. In most places it was low enough to enable them to step straight ashore, but towards the northerly or right-hand end, which was the end farthest from the island, it rose gradually to a maximum height of about ten or twelve feet. At this spot the rock, for the islet was little more than that, was some three hundred yards from the main island, but the other end, which tapered considerably, curved round until the tip was not more than thirty to forty yards from a spit of sand that jutted out from the beach, the sand deposit no doubt being caused by the islet's effect on the currents.

They pulled the boat into a fairly deep indentation in the rock and Biggles stepped ashore. For a moment he stood gazing at the island with speculative eyes. Then he turned back to Ginger.

'I think this place will suit us pretty well,' he observed, glancing around. 'The boat will ride here quite comfortably while you sit on the rock and keep an eye open for me to come back.'

'Right you are,' agreed Ginger. 'Where do you want me to put you ashore?'

'Anywhere on that beach will do,' replied Biggles, regarding a little sandy cove that lay immediately opposite the islet. 'It all looks the same, and there doesn't seem to be any one about.'

The final remark may have been induced by the fact that the moon was now clear above the horizon, flooding everything with its silvery light. The beach to which Biggles had referred lay clear and white, with hardly a ripple to mark the water-line, but beyond it and at each end the jungle towered up steeply to the usual central eminence, black, vague, and forbidding.

'Well, I might as well be getting ashore,' announced Biggles getting back into the boat, and pushing it out again into deep water. He picked up the oars, and a minute or two later the keel grated quietly on the soft sand of Elephant Island. 'Well, so long, laddie,' he whispered softly, getting out again. 'Keep awake; don't show a light, and above all don't make a noise.' Then, with a cheery wave, he set off at a brisk pace along the beach.

Ginger watched him until he was swallowed up in the dense shadows where the sand gave way to rock at the extremity of the bay. Then he turned his eyes on the primeval forest, silent, brooding, sinister, unchanged through the years, untouched by human hands, as far removed from the surging crowds of civilization as though it were on another planet. Apparently it slept—but only apparently. Within its sombre heart moved—what? Things. Things that crawled. Nameless horrors of a thousand legs and stings of death waging a perpetual warfare in the rotting tropic debris that cloaked the steaming earth. Larger things: panthers—sleek, black as the night through which they moved; pythons—twenty feet of sinuous horror; crocodiles of unbelievable size, survivors of another age that had outlived the centuries.

Ginger shivered, oppressed by a sudden pang of anxiety for Biggles. Then, knowing that he could do nothing to help him, he rowed back slowly to the islet.

Several hermit crabs scuttled into the sea as he backed the dinghy into the tiny creek that was not much larger than the boat, and stepped ashore. He did not tie the boat, for one reason because there was nothing to tie it to, and, as the water was almost motionless, there seemed to be no reason why he should. But he took the painter ashore, threw the end down near his feet, and, with his eyes on the pallid crescent of sand that fringed the bay, settled himself down to await Biggles's return.

A faint clicking noise made him turn again to the seaward side of the islet, and he saw that the crabs were coming back, crawling ashore on their ridiculous stilt-like legs in greater numbers than before. Some, already on the rock, were marching to and fro in small companies, for all the world like soldiers on parade. For a long while he watched them with interest, glancing from time to time at the beach, for there was something fascinating about the spectacle. Vaguely he wondered how long they had been carrying out their absurd exercises, and how long they would continue to do so.

Then, at last growing weary of them, he turned and watched the beach with a renewed interest, knowing that Biggles might return at any time. Occasionally a silver ripple would surge across the narrow strait that divided the islet from the island, a gleaming streak that threw up two little waves on either side of it, and he was thankful that swimming formed no part of the programme. He could not see, but he could guess what caused the ripples. And when, presently, a small fish shot high out of the water and he saw the huge grey shape that flashed beneath it, he knew that his suspicions were correct.

It was a little while after this that he became aware of something different. Something had changed. Something that had been there was no longer there. At first he could not make out what it was. But then, suddenly, he knew. The crabs were no longer doing their exercises. The bony clicking of their long legs had ceased, and quite casually he turned to see why.

A glance revealed the reason. They were no longer there. But it was not this simple fact that brought him to his feet with a startled cry. It was the discovery that the dinghy had drifted unaccountably away from its berth; already it was at the seaward end of the tiny creek, although fortunately the end of the painter still rested on the rock. But only just. He saw that in another moment it would be in the water, and he sprang forward quickly to pick it up; but even as he stooped, he stopped, staring. What was wrong with the boat? It seemed to be all lop-sided, as if a weight was pulling the side down into the water. He could see the weight, a dark, indistinct mass, hanging on the side of it. Then, as he stood staring, with his heart thumping strangely and his throat constricting, there was a swish in the air as of a rope when it is thrown. A dark, snake-like object curled through the air and fell with a soft thud across the rock on which he stood. It came so close that it grazed his ankle, and at the feel of it he leapt backwards, an involuntary cry of horror breaking from his lips.

He no longer thought of saving the boat. His only immediate concern was for his own preservation, and in a panic he ran towards the centre of the islet until, reaching what seemed to be a safe place, he turned and looked again. He was just in time to see the weight slide off the side of the dinghy, and the boat, thus released, right itself with a gentle splash.

His knees seemed to go weak, and he sank down limply on the rock, wondering with a sort of helpless horror how he was going to recover the boat now floating placidly some ten yards from the water's edge. To swim for it with that ghastly creature about was unthinkable. He knew what it was, of course: either an octopus or a decapod, perhaps the most loathsome living thing in all creation.

His anxiety was nearly as great as his fear. Without the boat he was helpless; what was even worse, Biggles would be helpless, too, when he arrived on the beach, and he might be expected at any moment. Yet he could do nothing except stand and stare in an agony of despair, clenching and unclenching his hands in his extremity. Then he saw something that once more put all thought of the boat out of his head. The octopus was crawling out of the water on to the rock.

For a second or two the horror of it nearly overwhelmed him, for he could see it clearly now; a great pig-like body as large as a barrel, with two long tentacles protruding in front and a number of shorter ones behind. A decapod. Indeed, so far did his nerves collapse that it was all he could do to prevent himself from screaming. He could only hope that the creature would not see him, for without the boat escape seemed to be out of the question; the mere thought of voluntarily entering the water in an attempt to swim to the island turned his skin to goose-flesh. He did not forget his automatic, but the weapon seemed hopelessly inadequate against such an adversary, quite apart from which he shrank from making a noise which could hardly fail to rouse the entire island to Biggles's undoing.

Then, farther down the islet, another of the creatures dragged itself out of the water, and began turning over pieces of rock as if searching for some sort of food that it expected to find underneath. At the same time the original decapod began to move slowly towards him, the two long tentacles groping with a soft slithering noise over the rocks in front of it.

Ginger fled. He dashed up the incline to the higher end of the islet, but a glance showed that there was no escape that way. To make matters worse, he saw that in another moment his pursuer would reach the foot of the slope and effectually cut off his retreat. He waited for no more, but in a condition that can only be described as blind panic, he tore back down the hill, leaping such obstructions as lay in his path, and raced to the narrow end of the islet, nearest to the island. Out of the corner of his eye he saw that the second horror had taken up the chase, and he distinctly heard its tentacles fall across the rocks behind him as he dashed past it.

Nearing the end of his run, a swift glance backward revealed both monsters not thirty yards behind, moving swiftly over the ground in a sort of rolling motion. The sight drove the last vestige of control from his paralysed faculties. He reached the absolute extremity of the islet, but he did not stop. A few yards away another rock, quite small, rose clear of the water, and he launched himself at it in a manner that in cold blood he would have regarded—quite properly—as suicidal. Miraculously he landed on his feet, and, stumbling to the top, he saw yet another rock, half submerged. Again he leapt.

This time he was not so lucky. The rock, which was almost awash, was covered with seaweed, and few things are as slippery as seaweed-covered rock. His feet landed squarely, but they shot away from under him, and he ricochetted sideways into the water. He was up in a flash, catching his breath in a great gasp, and was overjoyed to discover that he could stand on what seemed a hard, sandy bottom. Instinctively he made for the island, deliberately splashing and making as much turmoil as possible in the water. Twice he went under as he stumbled into deep channels, and had to swim a few strokes each time; but his objective was not far away, and almost before he was aware that he had reached it, he was dashing through a cloud of spray of his own making up the firm, sandy beach to the softer sand beyond. Then, and not before, did he stop to look behind him. All was silent; motionless except for the glowing ripples on the water that marked the course of his berserk passage. Of the decapods there was no sign, and so unreal did the whole thing seem at that moment that he almost fancied he had been the victim of a particularly vivid nightmare. The dinghy he could not see because, as he realized, it was on the other side of the islet.

Panting, he sank down on to the dry sand to recover his breath and as much self-control as he could muster, clenching his hands to stop the trembling of his fingers, for although the danger was past, the shock had left him weak and shaken. Human enemies were something he understood, a natural hazard only to be expected, encountered, and outwitted; but these dreadful creatures of the deep—

He brushed his hair back from his forehead impatiently and rose to his feet, peering in the direction of the islet in the hope of seeing the boat drift beyond the end of it, for his only chance of recovering it was, he knew, the rather forlorn one of a current or slant of air carrying it to the shore.

Nothing would have induced him to go back into that monster-haunted water in the hope of retrieving it, not even the knowledge of what the result of losing it might mean to Biggles as well as himself. There were, he discovered, limits to what he was prepared to do for the success of their enterprise, although only a few hours before he would have denied hotly any such imputation.

He derived a modicum of comfort from the thought that perhaps the tide might bring the boat in to the shore, and he watched the water-line for some minutes trying to make out whether the water was advancing or receding. The wavelets were, he observed, a little below the high-water mark indicated by the usual line of seaweed and shells, but whether the water was advancing or receding he could not discover, for there was little or no movement.

It dawned upon him suddenly that, standing as he was in the middle of the white beach, he was exposed to the gaze of any living creature, human or animal, that might be prowling about, which, in the circumstances, was hardly wise. The nearest and easiest cover for him to reach was, of course, the jungle that rose up behind him like a great black curtain, but he regarded it with disfavour. The end of the bay where Biggles had disappeared was not very far away, and this made a much greater appeal, particularly as Biggles might reasonably be expected to return the same way as he had gone.

Without any loss of time, therefore, he set off towards it, and was presently relieved to find that, although the sandy beach petered out, it gave way to a sloping shelf of rock that rose gradually to a low cliff about fifty feet high and continued along the foreshore as far as he could see. The only vegetation on it consisted of a few stunted bushes and gnarled trees, which suited him very well, for these enabled him to conceal himself, yet at the same time permitted a clear view of the beach, besides giving a fairly open aspect of the cliff along which Biggles had presumably gone.

A little farther along a queer formation of small trees

attracted his attention, and towards these he made his way with the intention of taking up his stand amongst them, there to await Biggles's return. Accordingly he turned his steps towards them, only to find on closer inspection that the trees were even more unusual than he had at first realized. Indeed, they almost looked as if they had been arranged by human hands instead of being a perfectly natural growth. Generally speaking, they occurred in groups of three or four, although in a few cases there were only two. But it was not the trees themselves that made his eyes grow round with wonderment as he approached, but what lay on top of them.

Another few paces and he saw beyond all doubt that even if the trees were natural, the burdens they bore were not; they were obviously artificial, although whether they had been fashioned by men, birds, or animals, he had no means of knowing. It appeared that across the lower forks of the trees, normally some ten or twelve feet from the ground, had been laid other slender branches. Across these, at right angles, was a rough trellis-work of smaller branches, while on top had been piled a great mass of twigs not unlike a gigantic jackdaw's nest. But the nests were not round. They were rectangular, or roughly oval, being between seven or eight feet long but only two or three feet wide.

For some minutes he stood staring at this extraordinary phenomenon, completely perplexed. 'What the dickens is it?' he muttered, taking a few steps sideways in order to regard it from a new angle. 'Well, if birds built those, I only hope they're not at home, that's all,' he concluded, picking up a piece of loose rock and throwing it at the nearest 'nest'.

Nothing happened. The rock bounded back on to

the ground with a clatter, and again the deathly silence settled over the scene.

'Well, I give it up,' he murmured, seating himself on a convenient boulder from which he could keep watch in both directions. It was a lonely vigil, and before long he found himself wishing fervently that Biggles would return; moreover, he was worried to death about the loss of the boat, and he wondered uneasily what Biggles would have to say about it when he knew. From time to time an unpleasant musty odour tainted the still night air and did nothing to add to his comfort; indeed, once or twice the stench was so bad that a wave of nausea swept over him. Still, he did not attempt to find the source of it, supposing that it was some sort of corruption in the forest.

For a long time he sat, sometimes staring at the beach, sometimes gazing the other way, and occasionally watching the moonbeams flicker on the rippling water that stretched away from immediately below him to the distant horizon. He could see the islet clearly, but there was still no sign of the boat.

Suddenly his reverie was disturbed by a sound that brought him to his feet with racing pulses. At first he could hardly believe his ears; it was quite faint, but it increased rapidly in volume and there was no mistaking it. It was the deep, steady throb of a powerful engine, but far too slow and heavy for an aero engine, to the sound of which he was accustomed. In startled alarm, he turned swiftly to each point of the compass in turn, trying to locate the noise, but he could not; it seemed to be advancing over the ground from the direction of the forest—which was, of course, impossible. For a few unbelievable seconds it seemed to beat against his feet as though it were passing underneath him. Then, as though the door of an engine-room had been opened, the sound was magnified ten times, and welled up behind him. He was round in an instant, eyes wide open, lips parted, prepared almost for anything except what he actually saw.

Straight from the base of the low cliff on which he stood was emerging, very slowly, a black torpedo-shaped object. For five breathless seconds he stared at it uncomprehendingly; then, as the unmistakable conning-tower came into view, he understood everything and dropped flat, quivering with excitement but completely self-possessed. It was a submarine, under way, heading out to sea.

The heads and shoulders of two men protruded from the circular super-structure, and a few words of a strange foreign language floated up to him.

In silent wonderment he watched the sinister craft, tense with the knowledge that the secret of the enemy's base was now his. Like a great fish with its back awash, it held on its course, leaving a flashing wake of disturbed water behind it, growing quickly smaller as, once clear of the islet, it increased its speed. The sound became a throbbing purr, then died away altogether, and the scene reverted to its former condition.

Chapter 12
Elephant Island

When Biggles had left Ginger and set off along the beach, his direction was not a matter of choice. The jungle which enveloped the whole island like a shroud was, he knew from previous experience of similar islands, practically impenetrable by day, and to attempt to force a passage through it by night would be a physical impossibility, quite apart from the very real danger of an encounter with one of the deadly beasts that dwelt in it and the noise that such a method of progress would inevitably entail. It was for these reasons, then, that he followed the beach, although he was aware that had he been able to reach the hill in the middle of the island, it might have been possible to command a view of the whole coastline, including his objective, in whichever direction that might lie.

What sort of country lay at the end of the little bay where the beach terminated he did not know, so he could only hope that the vegetation would not be so dense as to bar his progress. On reaching it he found to his relief that the sand gave way to a rising rocky foreshore on which the jungle had only been able to fasten an insecure hold. Through this he made fast time, keeping as near to the edge of the cliff as possible and stopping occasionally to listen. Once or twice he heard sounds in the undergrowth which suggested that wild creatures were pursuing their nocturnal tasks or pastimes, but as far as humanity was concerned, there was nothing to suggest that he was not alone on the island. On the right was the sea, calm, silent, deserted, gleaming wanly in the eerie light of the young moon. To the left, the forest, dark, unscrutable, heavy with an atmosphere of menace.

In this manner he covered what must have been three or four miles, seeing and hearing nothing to arouse his suspicions. Nevertheless, he did not relax his caution. He noticed that the moon was now behind him, and realized that in following the curve of the coastline he was now facing a different direction, and was able to estimate that he must have traversed nearly a quarter of the circumference of the island. Looking ahead, he saw that the cliff rose still higher, but intervening was another small bay, smaller than the one on which he had landed, but otherwise precisely the same in appearance. It was as if a giant dredge had grabbed a great lump out of the rock.

He reached the point where the cliff sloped down to it, and paused to scrutinize the open area, but a few moments' investigation revealed it to be as deserted as the other. Stepping carefully from rock to rock, he hastened down the slope and jumped lightly on the sand at the base.

As he landed there was an unpleasant squelch, and he sank into it over the ankles. At the same time the ground seemed to quiver and press tightly round his feet. Even so, it was not until he went to take a pace forward that he realized that he was in the grip of a quicksand.

He perceived afterwards that, had he stood still, even for a few seconds, when first he stepped on to the sand, he would certainly have died the most dreadful of all deaths; but, fortunately, such was his haste that only a barely perceptible instant elapsed between the time he jumped down and the time he started to move on, to discover that his feet were held fast. To say that he 'discovered' this may not be the literal truth. There was no time to discover anything, for, instantly, he began to fall forward, as was inevitable in the circumstances.

Even as he fell, the thought, 'quicksands', flashed through his brain, but the frantic grab that he made at an overhanging shrub was purely instinctive.

He managed to catch hold of it and hang on. For a few desperate seconds, as he began to haul on the branch round which his fingers had closed, it was touch and go whether it would stand the strain, or break and precipitate him bodily into a death-trap; but it held, and with the crisis passing as his feet began to emerge from the treacherous sand, it was only a matter of another second before he lay gasping on the rock and not a little shaken.

For a short while he sat regarding the innocent-looking beach with cold, hostile eyes, memorizing the lesson he had just learned—that in the tropics it does not do to trust anything, however harmless it may appear. Then, drawing a deep breath, he prepared to resume his march.

This, he discovered to his dismay, was likely to be difficult, if not impossible, for the jungle ran right down to the sand and both appeared to be impassable. He tried to find a way through the fringe of the tangled vegetation, and to some extent succeeded, but then a deep ravine into which he did not feel inclined to venture barred further progress. So he returned to the rock from which he had started. Somewhat to his surprise, he found that it was possible to work inland by keeping to the most prominent outcrops of rock, and he reproached himself for not investigating this direction before, although, thinking it over, he knew that it was the innocent-looking beach that had lured him on at that particular point.

The ground now rose steeply and, to his great satisfaction, the vegetation opened out instead of becoming more dense as he expected; and a quarter of an hour's hard work enabled him to reach the peak of a fairly considerable hill, from which he was able to make a comprehensive survey of the whole island and its coastline. It was with the coastline that he was particularly concerned, for he supposed that a submarine base was hardly likely to be established anywhere except on the actual shore.

Quickly his eyes swept round the limited sea-board, but all he saw was a succession of beaches, screes, and cliffs. Mystified, he looked again, this time more carefully, but with the same result. At first he was incredulous and refused to believe it, and it took him the best part of ten minutes to convince himself that he was not mistaken.

'Well, that's that,' he mused fatalistically, concealing his disappointment even from himself. 'There doesn't seem to be any reason why I shouldn't have a smoke.' He took a cigarette from his case, tapped it thoughtfully on the back of his hand, and then lighted it. For a little while he lingered, surveying the landscape that was as destitute of life as on the day it had emerged from the sea in some remote age, wondering what the next move would be now that his plan had so completely fizzled out.

'Yet it's funny about those lines,' he soliloquized, thinking of the chart that had been taken from the junk. 'This must be a watering-place, or a half-way mark, or something of the sort, that's the only solution. Well, I'd better see about getting back.'

He turned away from the tree against which he had

been leaning at the precise moment that a perfectly aimed *kris** struck it with a vicious *zip*. Where it came from he did not know; nor did he stop to inquire. For one fleeting instant, hardly understanding, he stared at it in shocked amazement, the haft still quivering, the steel gleaming brightly in the moonlight. Then he bolted, ducking as he ran.

Out of the corner of his eye he saw a number of figures take shape, flitting through the trees like shadows not ten yards distant, and he swerved like a hare away from them. He did not waste time feeling for his automatic; his assailants were too numerous and too scattered. Time for that when he was cornered or overtaken, he thought, as he sprinted down the hill towards the cliff.

Shouts now broke out behind him, and he hoped fervently that Ginger would hear them and take them as a warning to be prepared to move quickly when the crucial moment arrived and he reached the beach—if he did manage to reach it. Dodging, twisting, ducking, and jumping, he sped on. Reaching the cliff, he turned sharply to the right and set off back along the way he had come, but in a very different manner. For some time he did not look behind him, but concentrated his entire attention on avoiding the numerous obstacles that crossed his path; but reaching a fairly open space just before the point where the cliff began to slope down to the beach, he risked a quick glance over his shoulder.

What he saw made him redouble his efforts, for his pursuers were in a bunch not fifty yards behind. He looked again as he reached the far side of the open space, and saw to his horror that they were even closer,

* Small curved knife.

apparently travelling faster than he was now that the way lay open and the quarry was in view.

Biggles gathered himself for a final spurt. A dead branch protruded like a paralysed arm from a tree in front, and he ducked. In doing so he failed to see a loose rock that lay directly in his path. The first he knew about it was when his toe struck against it. Stumbling, he made a tremendous effort to save himself, but to become unbalanced at the speed he was travelling could have only one ending. For a split second he still ran forward, arms outstretched, and then crashed heavily to the ground.

Chapter 13
A Gruesome Refuge

Ginger was still lying on the cliff staring out to sea at the point where the submarine had disappeared when he heard another sound that brought him to his feet with a rush. It was a confused hubbub of several voices shouting at once, calling to each other. It sounded unpleasantly like an alarm, and if this supposition was correct, it seemed extremely likely that Biggles had had something to do with it—as was in fact the case. And when, a few seconds later, the shouting died away, only to be replaced by the drumming beat of running footsteps coming in his direction, his fears became acute.

Still, he did not lose his head. In any case it was no use running, for, with the boat gone, there was nowhere in particular to run to, so he took the obvious course, which was to find a hiding-place. The huge nests on their prop-like supports suggested themselves immediately, and up the nearest one he went without further loss of time. He was conscious of an overpowering stench as he clambered up on to the structure at the top and lay flat, but he ignored it, for his attention was entirely taken up by the hue and cry coming nearer every second.

Soon the chase came into view. Sprinting along the lip of the cliff, jumping over loose rocks, and swerving round trees and bushes, came Biggles. After him, with the relentless determination of a pack of wolves, came a mob of Dyaks, or tribesmen of some sort; the distance and the deceptive light made it impossible for Ginger to make out just what they were. Nor did he care particularly. As far as he was concerned, the fact that they were in hot pursuit of Biggles was all that mattered. And Biggles was sprinting for dear life towards his only hope of escape—the boat. There was no doubt of that. But the boat was not there!

It may have been the realization of this appalling fact that kept Ginger tongue-tied. His usual alert faculties seemed to be paralysed. What to do he did not know, and the very urgency of the situation only made him worse. In fact, he floundered in a horrible condition akin to stage-fright when he could only stare, incapable of lucid thought or action. Should he shoot? If he did, Biggles would probably stop, or at least hesitate, and that was something he could ill afford to do. Yet if he, Ginger, remained silent, Biggles would dash off down to the beach, only to find that there was no boat and no Ginger. What would he do then?

These were the thoughts that rushed through Ginger's brain as he watched the chase approach, but they did not occur in sequence. Rather were they a chaotic jumble of impressions—detached, incoherent.

Then, at the precise moment that Biggles drew level with the eyrie on which he was perched, so many things happened together that the result was pure nightmare. It began when Biggles caught his foot against a rock and took such a header that a moan of horror burst from Ginger's dry lips, and unconsciously he started forward in order to see if Biggles had hurt himself badly, as seemed by no means improbable. But either the sticks that comprised the 'nest' were rotten, or else the structure had not been designed for such treatment, for with a sharp cracking noise, the whole thing began to slip.

Ginger's reaction was purely automatic. Quite naturally he clutched at the sticks to save himself, and he sent a fair number of them flying in all directions before he succeeded. His fingers closed over something soft, and simultaneously a stench at once so awful, so nauseating, so completely overpowering filled his nostrils that he looked down to see what he was holding.

What he saw can safely be described as the final straw that broke the back of his already overwrought nerves. Staring up at him was a face: a human face—or what had once been a human face. It had not been a pretty thing to look at in life. In death it must have been awful, but in the advanced stages of decomposition it was so utterly dreadful that any description of it would fail in its object.

Ginger stopped breathing as he stared down into the glassy eyes and the grinning mouth with its protruding teeth. He forgot where he was. Forgot what he was doing. Forgot what was going on below. Forgot everything. He even forgot Biggles. A screech of stark terror broke from his lips as he sprang upright, arms waving as he strove to balance himself. Then he jumped clear. He was not in the least concerned about where he landed, or how. Had a famished lion been underneath he would have jumped just the same, for there was only one thought in his mind, which was to vacate the gruesome sepulchre on which he had taken refuge with all possible speed regardless of any other consideration.

Subconsciously he was aware of a number of men recoiling away from the spot, of a confused noise of shrieks and groans; then he struck the ground.

For a moment he lay still with the breath knocked out of him; then he staggered to his feet, swaying, glaring wildly about him. Not a soul was in sight. The men were gone. Biggles had gone. He was quite alone.

It seemed impossible, but there was no doubt about it. He was still staring, trying to force his brain to comprehend that this was in fact the case, when, without warning, his recent refuge collapsed completely, throwing its grisly tenant clear on to the rocks.

If Ginger had needed an incentive to cause him to move, nothing could have succeeded better. With a noise that was something between a moan and a yell, he turned on his heel and made a bee-line for the beach. Biggles's flight had been in the nature of a headlong rush, but it was not to be compared with Ginger's, which was stark panic.

But it did not last long. Rounding a corner at the point where the rock sloped down to the sand, he met somebody coming in the opposite direction. There was no time to dodge. There was no time to do anything. They met head on, and the result was instantaneous and inevitable. Ginger skidded sideways like a rugger ball on a greasy field, and collapsed with a crash into a convenient clump of bushes. Threshing and plunging like a salmon in a net, he fought his way out of the tangle, and then stopped dead, staring at Biggles, who was still sitting where he had fallen, muttering under his breath and rubbing his knee.

Ginger's relief was beyond words. 'Come on, Biggles,' he cried hoarsely. 'Let's get out of this perishing place.'

'That's what I'm aiming to do,' answered Biggles savagely. 'Where's the boat?'

Ginger faltered. 'There isn't one,' he muttered miserably.

'What do you mean—there isn't one?'

'It's—it's gone.'

'Gone! Who took it?'

'Nobody took it—I mean, it sort of went.'

'Went? Have you gone crazy?'

'An octopus took it,' explained Ginger.

'Don't talk such blithering nonsense,' snapped Biggles crossly. 'Are you asking me to believe that an octopus got into our boat and rowed it away?'

'No—that is, not exactly. You see—'

'Just a minute, just a minute,' broke in Biggles. 'Let me get this right. The boat's gone—is that it?'

'Exactly.'

'Fine!' muttered Biggles grimly. 'Now we know where we are. In a minute you can tell me how you came to lose it. Meantime, let's get down to the beach, or anywhere away from here, in case these pole-cats come back.'

'I frightened them, didn't I?' asked Ginger, as they hurried down to the beach.

'No! Oh, no! Frightened isn't the word. Supposing you were walking through a churchyard one night and a corpse pushed its tombstone over and leapt out at you with a yell—would you be frightened? I mean, you wouldn't stop to ask it questions?'

'No,' declared Ginger emphatically. 'I certainly should not.'

'Precisely!'

'But was that place a churchyard?'

'What goes for one in these islands. If they buried their dead, which couldn't be very deep on account of the primitive tools they've got, the crocs would dig them up. So they hoist them up in the trees. You must have found an empty grave.'

'Like fun I did,' snorted Ginger. 'He was at home all right, only I didn't see him when I first climbed up; you can bet your life on that. That yell you heard was me making his first acquaintance—ugh!'

'I don't wonder those fellows who were after me were

scared,' muttered Biggles, smiling at the recollection. 'I don't mind admitting that I was as shaken as they were, as you'd well believe if you'd seen me hoofing it as soon as I could get on my feet. But by the time I'd got down here I'd worked out what it was, and started back to fetch you. Wait a minute. I think this will do for a hide-out while we discuss what we're going to do.'

They had reached the beach, but instead of following the water-line, they worked their way to the edge of the jungle and pulled up in the inky shade of a giant casuarina tree.

'Now, then. Just tell me what happened,' invited Biggles. 'But make it short. It is known by now that there is at least one stranger on the island, and unless I've missed my guess, it won't be long before search parties are on the move.'

'They'll never find us in this darkness,' declared Ginger optimistically.

'Maybe not, but they'll watch every landing-place since they must know that whoever is here came by boat.'

'By the way,' asked Ginger suddenly, remembering the reason for the excursion and what he himself had seen, 'did you see any submarines?'

Biggles looked at him sharply. 'No,' he said. 'Nor did I see any place where one might expect to find one.'

'I have,' Ginger told him.

Biggles started. 'You've what?' he gasped.

'Seen a submarine.'

'Where?'

'Just along past the end of the bay—over there,' Ginger pointed.

'What, by that cliff!'

'The sub came out the cliff.'

'Came *out* of it—talk sense.'

'I am. I tell you I saw a submarine come out of the cliff and put out to sea. There must be a hole there—a cave of some sort.' Briefly, Ginger described how he had first heard and then seen the under-water craft, and followed this up by describing his adventures from the time the first decapod had dragged the boat away from the islet.

'My gosh! You have had a night of it,' muttered Biggles when he had finished. 'No wonder you were getting a bit het up when you bumped into me. Well, what are we going to do? This is the place we're looking for, there's no doubt about that, but the information isn't going to be much use to us unless we find a way of getting back to our rendezvous.'

'Could we make a raft, do you think?' suggested Ginger hopefully.

Biggles regarded him sadly. 'Have you ever tried to make a raft?' he asked.

'Never.'

'Then don't. I did once. Oh, yes, I know it sounds easy in books, but don't you believe it. Anyway, quite apart from that, I don't fancy rafting about on an octopus-infested sea. A liner wouldn't be too big for me after what you've just told me. All the same, things are not going to be too cheerful on this island now we've been discovered; except for that I wouldn't mind staying and lying low for a bit. But as soon as these johnnies have recovered from their fright they'll be back, and I don't like the look of the weapons they carry.'

'What sort of weapon is it?'

'A thing called a *kris*—a cross between a cutlass and a cleaver. Nasty.'

'Hadn't they got firearms?'

'Apparently not, or they'd have had a crack at me.'

'What happened?' inquired Ginger. 'I mean how did you come to barge into them?'

In a few words Biggles described his adventure. By the time he had finished the sky was beginning to turn grey, and he peered apprehensively along the beach.

'Look here, it's beginning to get light,' he muttered. 'We'd better find a better hiding-place than this in which to spend the day. First of all, though, let's make sure there's no chance of getting the boat. If we can get on to that rising land farther along to the right we ought to be able to see beyond the islet. Come on, let's go and have a dekko. Keep your eyes skinned.'

Chapter 14

Where is the *Seafret*?

They set off along the beach, keeping as close to the edge of the jungle as possible. Biggles broke into a steady trot as soon as he saw the coast was clear, for the day was fast dawning, and in this way they soon reached the end of the bay, where the vegetation, curving round to meet the sea, brought them to a halt.

'Come on, we shall have to force a way through this stuff,' muttered Biggles, plunging into the undergrowth in order to reach the top of the high ground of which he had spoken.

The going was heavy, and several times they were compelled to make detours around fallen trees with their hosts of clinging parasites; but in due course, panting and dishevelled, they reached the crest and looked down.

A cry of triumph at once broke from Biggles's lips, and Ginger murmured his satisfaction, for there, high and dry on even keel on the sand just round the headland, where the flowing tide had apparently cast it, lay the dinghy.

'We'd better go and get it,' said Biggles quickly. 'If any one comes along we shall lose it for good.'

Again they set off, this time downhill, in the direction of the boat.

'What are we going to do with it?' asked Ginger as they reached it, and saw with relief that it was undamaged, with the oars still in place.

Biggles thought swiftly. 'We ought to get out behind

the islet, as we arranged,' he answered, 'but I must say that I am tempted to go and have a look at this place where the submarine came out. There must be a cave or a hidden creek there. It's a bit risky, but we've got to have a look at it sometime to see just what there is there. It's no use trying to blow up the whole blessed island, and we might go on bombing the trees for weeks without hitting the vital spot.'

'Well, if we're going, no time could be better than this, I imagine,' suggested Ginger.

'How long will it take us to get there?'

'About five minutes. Certainly not more than ten. It's only just across the other side of the bay.'

'Come on, then, let's have a shot at it,' decided Biggles, well aware of the desperate nature of the enterprise. But, as he had just observed, they would have to look at it at some time or other, and they could not hope for a better opportunity than the present.

They pushed the boat into the limpid water and scrambled aboard. Biggles picked up the oars, and in a few seconds they were skimming towards their objective, keeping close in to the shore in order, as far as possible, to avoid observation.

Reaching the far side of the bay, Biggles rested on his oars while the dinghy crept forward under its own way round the rocky headland. For a moment or two he looked ahead eagerly, expectantly; but then a look of blank wonderment spread slowly over his face as he stared at a plain wall of rock. Not a cleft or a cave showed anywhere in the cliff; from the rank green vegetation fifty feet above to the turquoise ripples at their own level, the wall fell sheer without an unusual mark of any sort.

Turning, he looked at Ginger with questioning eyes.

'Well, what do you make of it?' he asked, a faint hint of scepticism in his voice.

Ginger was nonplussed. Never in all his life had he felt so foolish. 'I don't know what to make of it and that's a fact,' he admitted.

'You're not going to try to persuade me that a submarine sailed straight through that chunk of rock?'

Ginger shook his head. 'No,' he said. 'That's solid enough. Nothing but an earthquake could shift it.'

'Well, what's the answer?' inquired Biggles, a trifle coldly.

'A lemon, by the look of it,' smiled Ginger, weakly.

'You're sure this is the right place?'

'Absolutely certain.'

'In that case, it looks as if we've gone back to the age of miracles,' declared Biggles sarcastically, dipping the oars into the water.

'What are you going to do?'

'I'm going back to the islet. There's no sense in sitting here gazing at a blank wall; there's a degree of monotony about plain rock that I find distinctly boring.'

Not another word was spoken while Biggles rowed back across the bay and took the dinghy behind the islet so that it was concealed from the main island.

'Don't forget that this place is alive with octopuses,' warned Ginger.

'Don't you mean octopi?' suggested Biggles.

'What does it matter?' protested Ginger. 'Had you been here last night and seen them you wouldn't have stopped to consult your pocket dictionary, I'll bet.'

'I think it would be safe enough during daylight.'

'What about when it gets dark?'

'We shall be gone by then,' answered Biggles. 'Let's haul the dinghy ashore; we can forget all about it then and pass the day in the shade of that rock.' He nodded towards the mass of rock that rose at the higher end of the islet.

The rest of the day was in the nature of a picnic. The sun shone brightly, but a little breeze from the sea tempered the heat to a pleasant temperature, while the food and water Sullivan had put into the boat staved off the pangs of hunger. For some time they talked of the mystery of the submarine. Biggles was sceptical and made no secret of it, and at the end even Ginger began to doubt himself.

'The fact is, you didn't see a submarine at all; you only thought you saw one,' concluded Biggles.

After lunch they slept in turn, one keeping watch while the other rested, but not once did either of them see or hear anything of the men who they knew must be somewhere on the island.

'I should say they were a tribe of seafaring Dyaks,' decided Biggles at last, as the sun began to sink towards the western horizon. 'The locals in these parts are a wild lot, I believe, and would murder any one for a pair of boots. It begins to look to me as if we're all at sixes and sevens, and the people we're looking for aren't on this island at all, but—Strewth! What's that?'

He leapt to his feet with undignified haste as an aero engine roared—almost in their ears, it seemed. Ginger sprang round as if he had been stung, and peeping round the rock, they beheld a sight so inexplicable that for a time they could only stare speechlessly. Floating on the blue surface of the translucent water at the far end of the bay, the reflection of her silver image distorted beneath her, was a small seaplane. How it had got there without being heard or seen was a mystery that defied all logical conjecture. Not that they had time to contemplate the matter calmly, for, with a roar that sent the parrots screaming into the air, the aircraft sped across the water in a cloud of glittering spray and soared into the sky.

Biggles dragged Ginger down with him as he flung himself flat. 'What do you know about that?' he gasped.

'About what?'

'That seaplane.'

'Seaplane! You didn't see a seaplane—you only thought you saw one,' mocked Ginger, getting his own back for Biggles's gibe earlier in the day.

The machine flashed across their field of vision, climbing for height, and hardly knowing what to say, they watched it until it was a mere speck in the blue. Then the hum of the engine died away suddenly, and they saw it coming down again.

'He's been up for an evening reconnaissance, I should say,' observed Biggles quietly. 'Not a bad idea, either. The fellow in that machine would be able to see fifty miles in all directions from his altitude—a lot better than scouting about in a boat.'

'Maybe he was looking for the junk,' suggested Ginger.

'Quite likely,' agreed Biggles. 'Look out! Keep your face down. You can see a face looking up at you easier than you can see a hundred men with their faces covered.'

Out of the corners of their eyes they watched the machine glide in, saw its long floats kiss the water and run to a stop not fifty yards from the cliff. There was a bellow of sound as the engine roared again and the machine disappeared behind the headland. The noise of the engine ceased, and they waited for it to start again, but in vain. Once more silence settled over the scene, now mauve-tinted with the approach of twilight.

Biggles started collecting the belongings that were scattered about at their feet.

'What's the programme?' asked Ginger.

'I'm moving off,' said Biggles quietly.

'That suits me,' declared Ginger warmly. 'It's getting near octopus time.'

As is usual in the tropics, night closed in around them swiftly, and by the time they were ready to depart it was nearly dark.

'Which way?' asked Ginger, taking his seat in the boat.

'I'm going to have another look at that cliff,' announced Biggles.

'You won't be able to see much in this darkness.'

'Enough, I fancy.'

Just what he expected to find Biggles did not say, but he expressed no surprise when the dinghy rounded the headland and the secret of the seaplane's disappearance was explained—as was the case of the submarine. Gaping in the face of the cliff, low down on the waterline, was a great black hole like the mouth of a tunnel.

'Fancy not thinking of that! Why, a half-wit would have spotted it,' grunted Biggles disgustedly.

'Spotted what?'

'That there was a cave, exposed at low water, but submerged at high tide. It was high water when we came round here this morning.'

'Pretty good,' was Ginger's vague reply. Whether he was referring to Biggles's solution of the problem or the cave itself was not clear. 'Are you going to have a peep in?' he added.

'No. I'd like to,' confessed Biggles, 'but I don't think it would be good generalship. We've got the secret now, and it's up to us to pass it back to Sullivan before we take any more risks, so that he can send the information back to the people at home in case anything unpleasant happens to us. After we've done that we'll certainly come back and have a snoop round, because then our precious lives won't be of such vital importance if we get into a jam.'

'You speak for yourself,' growled Ginger.

Biggles laughed softly as he pulled on the oars, and the island faded into the dark background.

'Are you going to look for Sullivan?' asked Ginger.

'I am,' declared Biggles tersely.

'We shall be a bit early.'

'No matter. It's no use blinking at the fact that we've had a bit of luck in spotting this dug-out, and I'm itching to get the information off my chest before anything happens to upset our apple-cart.'

'What can happen?'

'Don't ask riddles. How do I know? But it's time you knew that on these jaunts of ours something usually does happen at the crucial moment to throw things out of gear.'

Ginger said no more, but prepared to make himself as comfortable as possible during the wait.

In the pitch darkness, with nothing to do once they had reached the rendezvous, the time seemed to pass slowly.

'Time he was here,' muttered Biggles at last, staring into the gloom to seaward.

Another quarter of an hour passed and Biggles stirred uneasily. 'Funny,' he said, as if to himself. 'I suppose we couldn't by any chance have missed him?'

Ginger said nothing. Biggles had expressed his own thoughts and he had nothing to add.

The next half-hour was the longest either of them could ever remember. 'Begins to look as if I was right,' Biggles observed dispassionately, at last.

'How so?'

'About things going wrong.'

'But surely nothing could go wrong with the destroyer?'

'Then why isn't it here?'

'That, I admit, is something I can't answer,' was Ginger's only comment.

Another half-hour or so elapsed, and Biggles roused himself from the listening position in which he had been sitting. 'I don't think it's much use waiting here any longer,' he announced bitterly. 'Sullivan isn't coming, or he'd be here by now.'

Ginger barely heard the last part of the sentence. He had crouched forward in a rigid attitude, listening tensely. 'Hark!' he said softly. 'I can hear something. What is it?'

From somewhere far away out to sea a deep drone pulsed through the night; for a moment or two it persisted, rising to a crescendo, and then died away. A moment later the sound was repeated, and then again, slightly louder.

'What does that sound like to you?' asked Biggles in an odd tone of voice.

'If I were near a naval airport I should say it was a marine aircraft, taxi-ing over water,' replied Ginger slowly.

'Yes, I think you've hit the nail on the head,' agreed Biggles.

'You mean—'

'It's Algy taxi-ing here to fetch us. Something has happened to the destroyer.'

Ginger felt his heart go down like a lift. 'By gosh! I hope you're wrong for once,' he muttered anxiously.

'Well, we shall see,' was Biggles's pessimistic reply. 'One thing is certain,' he went on, as the sound moaned through the night comparatively near at hand. 'It's an aircraft, and if it isn't Algy we shall shortly be in the cart—up salt creek without a paddle, as the sailors say.'

The sound drew nearer, and it was quite easy to follow what was happening. Some one was sitting in the cockpit of an aircraft opening up the engine and easing back the throttle each time the machine gathered way.

'We don't want him to run us down,' exclaimed Biggles suddenly, rising to his feet.

He waited for one of the intermittent silences, and then, cupping hands round his mouth, let out a moderately loud hail.

A call answered them immediately. The recognized Algy's voice and rowed towards it, and a minute later the dark silhouette of the *Nemesis* loomed up in front of them. Biggles urged the dinghy forward until its bow was chafing the hull of the amphibian just below the cockpit.

Algy's head appeared over the side. 'Hello!' he said, switching off the engines.

'Hello yourself,' returned Biggles grimly. 'What in thunder do you think you're doing, buzzing about on the high seas? Where's the *Seafret*?'

'She was torpedoed this morning—at least, that's what it looked like.'

Biggles turned stone cold. 'Good heavens!' he ejaculated. 'Was she sunk?'

'No, Sullivan managed to beach her.'

Biggles balanced himself in a standing position. 'Tell me about it—quickly,' he invited.

'Nothing much to tell,' answered Algy simply. 'The *Seafret* was sitting in the little bay at Hastings Island—at anchor, of course. I had taxied the machine on to the beach and was giving her a look over when I was nearly knocked flat by an explosion. When I looked up I saw a cloud of smoke hanging over the destroyer. She had already taken on a bad list. Sullivan slipped his cable and ran her straight ashore not fifty yards from where I was.'

'No lives lost?'

'No.'

'Thank God for that, anyway. What's Sullivan doing?'

'Sitting on the beach cursing mostly. They've got plenty of stores ashore and have made a camp.'

'By heaven! These people must be pretty desperate to do a thing like that; any one would think they were deliberately trying to start a war.'

'Not necessarily,' replied Algy. 'As Sullivan says, who's to say it was a torpedo? Nobody saw anything, either before or after the explosion. He says that in the ordinary way if he went home and said he'd lost his ship because she'd been torpedoed the Admiralty would laugh at him. People don't fire torpedoes in peace time.'

'Don't they, by James!'

'We know they do, but it would be hard to prove, particularly as we don't know whom to accuse of doing it.'

'That's true enough,' admitted Biggles. 'So Sullivan's still at Hastings Island?'

'Yes, and he's likely to be for some time.'

'Hasn't he called for assistance by wireless?'

'No. We decided that the enemy would pick up the SOS as well as our own people, so it might be better to lie low and say nothing for a day or two. We had a conference, and came to the conclusion that the first thing to do was for me to fetch you.'

'Quite right,' agreed Biggles. 'Did you see anything of the submarine yourself?'

'Not a thing. I did think of taking off and trying to spot it, but what was the use? I couldn't have done anything even if I had seen it, and had they come to the surface and seen me, they would then have known that I was there. As it was I don't think they could have suspected the presence of an aircraft. They just lammed a "mouldy" into the destroyer and made off.'

'Yes, I suppose that was about the size of it,' admitted Biggles.

'Well, if you'll get aboard we'll see about getting back.'

'Just a minute—not so fast,' protested Biggles. 'Let me think.'

For a little while he leaned against the side of the amphibian deep in thought. When he moved, his mind was made up. 'No,' he said, 'I'm not going back with you.'

'You're *not*?'

'No.'

'What are you going to do?'

'Stay here. Listen, this is how things stand. Memorize what I say because you may have to repeat it to Sullivan. Elephant Island is the place we've been looking for. In the central face of rock on the eastern side—almost opposite us now—there is a cave. What it leads to I don't know, but inside there are submarines and aircraft. We've seen them both. If it's an underground lake, or something of that sort, then it's no earthly use bombing it from above. That's why we've got to find out what it is. The entrance is covered at high water, so whatever we do will have to be done at low tide. This is my idea. The tide is down now. As soon as the moon comes up Ginger and I will get into the dinghy and go and have a look at this underground war depot. You stay here, or better still, get behind the islet so that you can't be seen from the shore, but don't get too close to the rock or you may find an octopus in the cabin when you go to take off. And don't make more noise than is necessary. They may have heard you for all we know, but it can't be helped if they have. Well, how does that strike you as a programme?'

Algy hesitated. 'I can't say that I'm exactly enamoured of it,' he confessed, dubiously. 'I suppose it's imperative that you should go poking about in this cave?'

'Absolutely,' declared Biggles. 'What is the alternative—if any? As I see it, the whole Far East fleet of the Royal Navy could hammer away at the island for weeks without hurting these submarine merchants more than giving them a slight headache from the noise. More direct methods will be demanded to hoist them skyward, but until we know just what we've got to destroy it is difficult to know how to apply them.'

'Yes, I see that,' admitted Algy. 'But what is Sullivan going to think when we don't turn up.'

'He'll have to think what he likes.'

'I hope he won't do anything desperate.'

'So do I—but there, we can't let him know, so we shall have to take a chance on it.'

'All right,' agreed Algy. 'If you're satisfied, then it's OK by me. Let's get the *Nemesis* to this islet you talk about. Do you know where it is?'

'Pretty well. Throw me a line. We'll tow the machine there—it isn't far. I'd rather you didn't start the engines again.'

The moon rose as they towed the *Nemesis* into position, and the final disposition of the aircraft behind the high shoulder of rock was made with some haste, for

Biggles was frankly nervous about their being seen or heard by those on the island. It was not their personal safety that concerned him so much as the possible failure of their plans, for, as he pointed out to the others, with the aircraft at their disposal, ready to start at a moment's notice, if the worst came to the worst, they could always take flight with every prospect of getting away.

'Has any one got the time?' he asked, as the *Nemesis* dropped her small anchor in thirty feet of water.

'A few minutes short of midnight,' answered Algy, glancing at his instrument board. 'Are you going to move off right away?'

'No, I don't think so,' answered Biggles. 'The hour before dawn has acquired a reputation through the ages for being the best time to catch people napping, and for all nefarious enterprises. I'll wait for a bit. Pass me down a torch, will you; we shall probably need one.'

Algy went through into the cabin and fetched a small electric torch, which he handed down to Biggles, who was still standing in the boat. 'Anything else you want?' he asked.

'No, I think that's everything,' replied Biggles slowly. 'We've got guns, but I don't think we shall need them—anyway, I hope not. With luck, to-morrow will see the end of this business, and I can't say I shall be sorry,' he added thankfully.

Two hours later he embarked on one of the most desperate adventures of his career.

Chapter 15
Trapped!

A gentle breeze, bringing with it the subtle aroma of spices, caused the water to ripple and gurgle softly against the prow of the dinghy as, under the stealthy impetus of the oars, it edged round the headland and approached the cave which, as they drew near, they observed was larger than they had at first supposed. Except for the incessant lapping of the tiny wavelets against the rock, and the occasional distant, choking grunt of a crocodile, there was no other sound, yet to Ginger the atmosphere seemed charged with hidden threats and the presence of things unseen.

Inch by inch they approached their objective. Biggles dipped his left oar deeply, and the boat crept nearer to the cliff until Ginger, by reaching out, was able to touch it. Another minute and the bows projected beyond the opening; another, and they sat staring into a cavity that was as black as the mouth of the pit. Neither spoke, knowing full well that in such conditions the sound of the human voice travels far.

Another stroke of the left oar and the nose of the dinghy came round until it was pointing directly into the void; an even pull and they were inside, swallowed up in such a darkness as Ginger had never before experienced. It was not darkness in the ordinary accepted sense of the word, the darkness of a moonless night; rather was it an utter and complete absence of light, the darkness of total blindness.

A gentle click, and from the centre of the boat sprang

a beam of light that cut through the air like a solid white cone as Biggles switched on the torch. He regretted having to use it, but further progress without illumination of some sort was, he felt, quite useless, if not impossible. He realized that if guards had been posted they would see the yellow glow of a match as certainly as they would the more powerful beam of the electric torch, so he accepted the risk as inevitable, and switched it on, half prepared for the action to be followed immediately by a signal of alarm.

But all remained silent. Slowly the round area of light travelled over the walls, to and fro, above and below, but it revealed nothing except a semi-circular arch of rock with a floor of still, silent water, which appeared to run straight into the very heart of the island.

There was another click as Biggles switched off the light, and a moment later Ginger felt the boat moving forward again. It was an eerie sensation, gliding through space in such conditions. The only sound was the faint swish of the oars as they dipped in and out of the water, and he wondered how long Biggles would be able to keep the boat on a straight course. It was longer than he expected, and some minutes elapsed before the side of the dinghy grated gently on the rough wall. Thereafter progress was slower, for rather than switch on the light again Biggles began to maintain a forward movement by using his fingers against the wall, taking advantage of any slight projection that he could feel. As soon as he realized what was happening Ginger joined in the task.

It was difficult to estimate how far they travelled in this manner, but it must have been several minutes later when Ginger's warning hiss caused Biggles to desist, for, as he had been at the oars, his back was towards the bows, and he was unable to see ahead. Turning quickly, he saw at once what it was that had attracted Ginger's attention. Some distance in front, just how far he was unable to tell, a half-circle of wan blue light had appeared, and he realized that it was the end of the tunnel.

Quickly he pushed the boat clear of the wall, picked up the oars, and in two or three strokes had completely turned it round, whereupon he began backing towards the light, which he soon perceived was cast by the moon. His object in turning the boat was, of course, that the nose might be pointing in the right direction for speedy retirement should an alarm be given.

The nervous tension of the next few minutes was so intense that Ginger clutched at the gunwale of the boat to steady his trembling fingers, at the same time craning his neck so that he could see what lay ahead, for he felt that anything, *anything* might happen at any moment. Somewhat to his surprise, and certainly to his relief, nothing happened. With infinite slowness the boat floated backwards until it was possible to see through the opening at what lay beyond. At first, owing to the deceptive light, it was rather difficult to make out just what it was, but as they gazed section by section of the scene unfolded itself.

Biggles realized instantly that he was looking into an old crater, the crater of a long extinct volcano, now filled with water which had come through from the sea presumably by the same channel through which they themselves had come, and which had, no doubt, once been a blow-hole bored by a colossal pressure of pent-up gas when the rock had been in a fluid, or semi-fluid, state. The island itself must have been the actual peak of the volcano which, with the cooling of the molten mass, had remained hollow.

The sides of the crater were not very high; they dropped sheer from heights varying from one hundred to a hundred and fifty feet to sea-level, where, of course, the water began. At one place only, not far from where the dinghy floated, the wall had crumbled away until the slope, while steep, could easily be scaled, and was, he perceived, the path by which the submarine crews travelled to and from their quarters, which were situated half-way up the cliff. Even now the dark bulk of a submarine rested motionless against a rough quay at the base of the incline.

At the back of Biggles's mind as he took in these general impressions was a grudging admiration for whoever had discovered the place and thought of turning it into a submarine base, for as such it was more perfect than anything that could have been fashioned by human hands. Another point he realized was that even if he had flown over the island, while he might have seen the gleam of water, he would merely have taken it for a lake, for the buildings, being built of the actual rock which formed the sides of the crater, or camouflaged to resemble them—he could not tell which—would certainly have escaped detection.

These buildings he now examined in detail with the practised eye of an aerial observer. No lights were showing. There were four in all. The lowest three were long, squat structures, evidently living quarters or store-rooms; in fact, just the sort of accommodation one would expect to find. The top one, however, perched almost on the lip of the crater, was much smaller, square in shape, and he wondered for what purpose it was used until he saw the antennae of a wireless aerial outlined like a spider's web against the moonlit sky. That, so far as he could see, was all the information he would be able to pick up from an exterior view of the buildings.

There was only one object on the water besides the submarine already remarked. It was a seaplane which floated, with wings folded, near the foot of the path just beyond the underwater craft. It was easy to see how it was employed. It could not, of course, take off from the crater, but with its wings folded it could easily pass through the tunnel to the open sea where, with its wings rigged in flying position, it could operate at will.

There seemed to be nothing else worthy of note, and Biggles was about to turn away, well satisfied with his investigation, when Ginger, whose end of the boat had swung round somewhat, giving him a slightly different view, touched him on the elbow and pointed. At first Biggles could not see what it was that he was trying to show him, but a touch on the oars brought him in line, and he was just able to make out a narrow cleft, or opening, in the rock wall not more than a few yards from where they sat. A slight pull on the oars brought them to it; another, and they had passed through the gap and were staring with astonished eyes at what met their gaze. The place seemed to be a sort of secondary crater, very small, not much larger in area than a fair-sized house, but in this case the walls were perpendicular. It was quite a natural formation, if somewhat unusual, but Biggles was only interested in what he saw on the surface of the water. There was no possibility of mistake. The round, buoy-like objects, with horns projecting at different angles, could only be mines such as are used in naval warfare. A little farther on, as his eyes became accustomed to the gloom, he could just discern, packed on ledges of rock which looked as if they had been cut by hand, a vast array of metal cylinders with pointed ends, and he did not have to look twice to recognize them as shells.*

At this discovery the whole matter took a different turn. Not only was the place a submarine depot, but it seemed also that it was a naval armoury, an armament stores depot capable of supplying a fleet with material, to say nothing of laying a minefield around itself for its own protection. And the concentration of stores was apparently still proceeding, harmless-looking junks being used for the purpose. There was another dark area at the far end of the tiny crater which looked as if it might reveal further secrets, but Biggles had seen enough. He knew all he needed to know, and his one concern now was the destruction of the whole concern.

'My goodness! These people have got a brass face, if you like,' he breathed in Ginger's ear. 'Fancy having the nerve to put up a show like this on a British island!'

His eyes swept over the array of sinister-looking mines for the last time, and his oars were already in the water for immediate departure when an idea flashed into his head, so audacious that for a moment it took his breath away. Yet was it audacious? There was a submarine outside. Ginger had seen it go out. It could not have come back without their seeing or hearing it. It might return at any time. One mine in the tunnel! The submarine could not fail to strike it as it came in, whereupon, even if the tunnel did not completely cave in, as seemed likely, the submarine would sink in the fairway, effectually bottling up everything that was inside the crater. The R.A.F. machines could do the rest in their own time. All that was necessary was to place a mine in position, bolt back to the *Nemesis*, fly

* Artillery projectile, in this case for naval guns

to the *Seafret*, and call up the military machines from Singapore on the destroyer's wireless. The plan, if successful, would, he saw, be more certain and conclusive in its result than simply calling upon the Royal Air Force to bomb the place, when it was quite on the boards that one or both of the submarines would escape, possibly taking the personnel of the island with them to report to their headquarters what had happened and perhaps start a similar scheme somewhere else.

All this flashed through Biggle's head a good deal faster than it takes to read, and as he turned the plan over quickly in his mind he knew that he was going to put it into action.

'What's the idea?' whispered Ginger, who was watching him closely.

'I'm going to lay one of these mines in the tunnel,' declared Biggles, in the incisive tones he always used when he was keyed up for action.

'A sort of miniature Zeebrugge*, eh?' grinned Ginger.

'Exactly. Hang on while I see if these pills are fastened together. Don't run the boat against one of those spikes or we shall take a flight through space that will make Clem Sohn's show look like a half-fledged sparrow doing its first solo.'

The 'spikes' to which Biggles referred were, of course, the 'horns' of the mines, which, in effect, act like triggers, in that anything coming into contact with them depresses a firing-pin into a detonator, which explodes the bursting charge.

The mines were, Biggles quickly ascertained with

* British naval raid, April 1918, to block the two outlets of this German-occupied seaport and destroy installations.

satisfaction, merely roped together at equal intervals to prevent them from bumping against each other; and with far less trouble than he expected he untied one, and then ordered Ginger to 'hang on to it' while he picked up the oars.

Ginger obeyed promptly but without enthusiasm, for like most people who are unaccustomed to handling high explosive, he regarded any instrument containing it with deep suspicion and mistrust. However, leaning over the stern, he got his hand through the iron ring attached for that purpose, and in this position was rowed by Biggles back into the tunnel.

'Be careful you don't barge into the wall,' warned Ginger nervously. 'For the love of mike use your torch.'

'It's all right, you can let it go now,' replied Biggles. 'Don't worry; I hate the sight of these things as much as you do. Two minutes and we shall be out.'

Ginger released his dangerous charge with a deep sigh of relief, and could have shouted with joy when, a moment later, with Biggles bending to the oars, the entrance to the tunnel came into view. He was watching the pale grey opening become lighter as they drew nearer to it when, to his surprise, it was suddenly blotted out. At the same moment a deep, vibrant roar filled the tunnel, and he knew what it was.

'It's the submarine!' he cried in a strangled, high-pitched voice. 'She's coming in!'

Chapter 16
In the Lion's Den

That was, without doubt, one of the most desperate moments of their many desperate adventures. Biggles gasped out something—what it was Ginger did not hear—and whirling the dinghy round in its own length, set off back down the tunnel with all the power of his arms. A light flashed from the bows of the submarine and illuminated the cave as brightly as broad daylight. Then a shout rang out.

Biggles did not stop. Strangely enough, in his frantic haste to race the submarine he forgot all about the mine, and Ginger let out a shrill cry of horror as they missed it by a foot, their wake setting it bobbing and rolling in the middle of the fairway.

'Keep your head,' snarled Biggles angrily. 'I'm going to make for the quay—it's our only chance. Try and keep together . . . we've got to get up that path . . . use your gun if any one tries to stop you.'

They shot through the end of the tunnel into the moonlit crater, Biggles grunting as he threw his weight on the oars, knowing that life or death was going to be a matter of a split second. In his heart was a wild hope that they might reach the quay before the mine exploded, but it was not to be. He had just ascertained from Ginger that no lights were showing in the buildings when, with a roar like the end of the world, from the mouth of the tunnel belched a sheet of flame that shot half-way across the crater.

Biggles continued rowing without a pause, but there

was only time for two more strokes. Then something seemed to come up under the boat and carry it forward with the speed of a racing motor-launch. The oars went by the board as he clutched at the sides to prevent himself from going overboard; and before anything could be done to prevent it, the dinghy had crashed into the under-carriage of the seaplane with such force that the top was ripped clean off one of the floats and a hole torn in the dinghy's side. It began to sink at once. Ginger grabbed at the undamaged float and managed to drag himself across it. Biggles was not so lucky. He fell into the water, but managed to seize the end of the damaged float, to which he hung, trying to make out what was happening ashore. 'Hang on,' he choked. 'Don't show more of yourself than you can help.'

At the moment Ginger was far too concerned with keeping his place on his refuge to pay much attention to anything else, for around them the water boiled and heaved and foamed as, flung into a maelstrom by the explosion, it dashed itself against the cliff, only to be hurled back in a smother of spray to meet a wave receding from the opposite wall.

The effect of this on the heavy submarine was bad enough, for it rocked like a cork, rolling its metal plates against the quay with an appalling grinding noise; but the antics of the lightly floating seaplane were terrifying in their complete abandon. It reared and bucked and threw itself about like a newly roped wild horse, sometimes thrusting its propeller deep into the waves, and at others standing on its tail with half of its floats out of the water. Fortunately, this state of affairs did not last long, and once the first shock had passed the miniature tornado began quickly to subside.

But on the shore—if shore it could be called—things

were happening. From each of the three lower buildings men began to run down towards the quay, some shouting orders as they ran. Lights appeared everywhere.

'Looks like the evacuation of Sodom and Gomorrah,' grinned Biggles, his curious sense of humour overcoming all other emotions even at this critical juncture. 'I wonder what they think they're going to do.'

This was apparently something that the men themselves did not know, for they merely crowded on the end of the quay nearest to the cave, talking and gesticulating as they tried to ascertain the cause of the explosion.

Presently, when they had all collected there, Biggles realized that no better opportunity of escape would ever be likely to present itself. The tunnel had, he felt sure, caved in, or had so far become choked with debris as to be impassable. In any case they had no boat, so their only avenue of escape lay in the cliff path down which the men had come. It was, he knew, a forlorn hope at the best, but there was no other way, and their chances would certainly not be improved by the broad light of day which could not now be long in coming.

'Ginger,' he said quietly.

'Ay, ay, sir,' answered Ginger, with the calm that comes of knowing that things are so bad that they can hardly be worse.

'I'm going to make a dash for the top of the hill while these stiffs are all down on the quay,' Biggles told him. 'It's our only chance. If we can make the top we might, by taking to the jungle, get back to Algy. Are you ready?'

'OK, Chief.'

'Come on, then.'

They released their hold on the seaplane and swam the few yards to the nearest point where they could effect a landing. Unfortunately, it meant going nearer to the men clustered on the quay, but there was no other landing-place, for in the opposite direction the cliff fell sheer into the water.

At first their luck held. They dragged themselves ashore dripping like water-spaniels, and had actually succeeded in getting above the quay before one of the men, for no reason at all, apparently, happened to look round. Ginger, who had kept one eye on the crowd, saw him peer forward, evidently seeing or sensing something unusual in their appearance; he saw him call the attention of the next man, who turned sharply and looked at them. He in turn called out something which made several of the others look; then, with one accord, they started up the path. At first they only walked, but as Biggles and Ginger quickened their pace they broke into a trot. Biggles started to run, and that was the signal for the chase to begin in earnest. Above, the sky was already grey, flushed with the pink rays of dawn.

The climb would have been a stiff one at the best of times, being sharply sloping rock for the most part, with hand-hewn steps occurring in the worst places; to take it at a run called for considerable endurance, and before they had gone far both Biggles and Ginger were breathing heavily.

Biggles was thankful for one thing. It seemed that the entire population of the enemy camp had, as was not unnatural, rushed down to the quay to see what had caused the explosion, so there was no one to bar their path. Had there been, then their case would have been hopeless from the start.

Rounding a shoulder of rock in which a flight of steps had been cut, he saw something that brought an ejaculation of satisfaction to his lips. Beside the path, where the workmen had piled it rather than carry it away, was a stack of detritus, pieces of rock of all shapes and sizes, just as it had been cut out in the construction of the steps. He was on it in a flash, kicking and pushing with hands and feet. Ginger joined him, and a minor avalanche of rocks and dust went bouncing and sliding down the path.

There was a yell from below as their pursuers saw what was happening and dashed for such meagre cover as the causeway offered. Which was precisely what Biggles had hoped to achieve, for it gave them a fresh start of which they were not long taking advantage.

'We've done it!' he gasped, as they burst round the last bend and saw that they were not more than twenty yards from the top, with the enemy a good forty or fifty yards behind. But he spoke too soon, although it was not to be expected that he could foresee what was to happen next.

Over the brow of the cliff, beyond which they could just see the thatched, conical roofs of huts, poured a stream of Dyaks armed with their weapon, the *kris*, which, in the hands of an expert, can take a man's head from his shoulders as cleanly as a guillotine. Their appearance confirmed what Biggles had suspected the previous day, that the enemy had locals in their employment, brought possibly from their own islands in the China Sea.

There seemed to be only one hope left, and Biggles, without pausing in his stride, swerved towards it—the wireless building, a rock-built structure with a heavy door made of rough-hewn planks of island timber. Would the door open? If it was locked—

With Ginger facing the mob, gun in hand, he tried the door. It opened easily, and they both burst inside.

Two men, oriental in appearance, in gold-braided

blue uniforms, who had been sitting at the desk in front of a magnificent modern wireless equipment, sprang to their feet with startled eyes as the two airmen burst in. For an instant they stared, their dark eyes flashing from one to the other of the intruders; then the elder, his face with its high cheek-bones clouding with suspicion, pulled open a drawer and whipped out a revolver.

Biggles's pistol spoke first, and the man crumpled up like an empty sack.

The other darted round the desk with the obvious intention of getting to the door. Ginger barred his path, but at Biggles's quickly snapped, 'All right, let him go', he stood aside and the man disappeared.

Biggles slammed the door behind him, locked it, and slipped the bolt with which it was fitted. Then, with his back to it, his eyes swept the room. It was typical of him that the major issue still weighed more with him than personal considerations, as his next words showed, for he did not waste time discussing ways and means of escape from the trap in which they found themselves.

'Can you handle that set?' he rapped out.

'I don't see why not,' answered Ginger, reaching the apparatus in three quick strides.

'Then try and get Singapore—usual wavelength,' Biggles told him tersely. 'As soon as you get 'em let me know. If the *Seafret* interferes tell the operator to listen but not jam the air.' As he finished speaking Biggles threw up his automatic and blazed at a face that appeared at the only window the cabin possessed, a small square of light near the door. One of the panes flew to fragments and the face disappeared.

Ginger did not even look up; with the earphones clipped on his head, he was already revolving the black vulcanite controls.

Biggles took up his position close to him, facing the window, pistol ready for snap-shooting.

There was a short silence; then something crashed against the door. Occasionally a dark figure flashed past the window, but Biggles held his fire. Time was the one factor that mattered now. If he could hold the place until he had got a message through to Singapore he didn't care much what happened after that. He saw that it was now broad daylight, and he was wondering what Algy would be thinking, when there came a crash on the door that made the whole building shake. But it held. For how long it would stand up to such treatment he did not know, but obviously it could not last many minutes. Then, with a crackle as of wood being broken up with incredible speed, a stream of machine-gun bullets poured through it, sending a cloud of splinters flying across the room; but they were well out of the line of fire, and the shots spattered harmlessly against the opposite wall.

'Any luck?' he asked Ginger, quietly.

'I've got *Seafret*—strongly, too—but I haven't been able to hook up with Singapore yet.'

'Never mind Singapore then; give this message to Sullivan and ask him to transmit it as quickly as possible,' said Biggles quickly, taking a map from his pocket and opening it on the desk. For a second or two he studied it closely; then, picking up the pencil that had been dropped by the operator, he wrote swiftly on a message block, disregarding the attack on the door which was now being prosecuted with increasing vigour. When he had finished he pushed the slip over to Ginger, picked up his pistol again, and resumed guard over the window.

It was as well that he did so, for at that moment an arm, holding a revolver, appeared through the broken glass, and a bullet ploughed a long strip of leather from the top of the desk. Biggles leapt aside just in time, and before the man could fire again he had taken two swift paces forward and blazed at the arm from point-blank range. There was a yell outside; the revolver fell inside the room, and the arm was withdrawn.

'O.K.,' called Ginger. 'Sullivan's got the story. Have you anything else to say to him?'

'Tell him we're in a jam—'

'I've told him where we are.'

'That's fine. Tell him not to worry about us but get through to Singapore as quickly as he can.'

Ginger returned to his task, but a moment later looked at Biggles with puzzled eyes. 'That's funny,' he exclaimed.

'What is?'

'I was speaking to *Seafret* when the operator cut in and said, "Hang on! Stand by for—" And that's as far as he got when the instrument went stone dead. I can't get a kick of any sort out of it.'

'I should say they've cut the lead-in wire outside,' answered Biggles, without taking his eyes from the window. 'They'd be pretty certain to do that as soon as they realized that we might start broadcasting for help. I wonder what *Seafret* meant by telling us to stand by. What for? But there, it's no use guessing. I should like to know what's going on outside; they seem to have stopped banging on the door.'

'I suppose we can't hold out until the R.A.F. machines arrive?'

Biggles shook his head definitely. 'No,' he said. 'That's out of the question. They'll be hours. In any case, the last place we want to be when they start doing their stuff is here; believe me, life won't be worth living.' As he finished speaking, actuated by a sudden impulse, he snatched a quick glance through the window. It was only a momentary glimpse, but it revealed a lot. 'My goodness!' he gasped.

Standing in the middle of the path, not ten yards from the door and pointing towards it, was a machine-gun on a tripod, a metal belt of ammunition hanging out of it like a long flat centipede. There was nothing surprising about that; on the contrary, it was just what he expected to see; but he certainly did not expect it to be deserted. A little farther down the path a large party of men, some in uniform, and others, the Dyaks, bare-skinned, were dragging a much heavier gun into position. Scattered about the rocks in various positions watching the proceedings were others, mostly officers, judging by their uniforms.

Biggles made up his mind with the speed and precision that comes from long experience in the air. 'I'm going to make a bolt for it,' he snapped. 'Keep me covered as far as you can.' With that he unfastened the door, flung it wide open, and raced to the machine-gun.

It is probable that this was the very last thing the people outside expected. One does not look to a rabbit to leave its burrow voluntarily when a pack of terriers is waiting outside. Certain it is that not one commander in a hundred would have anticipated such a move, or made allowance for it. On the face of it, it was sheer suicide, but as so often happens in the case of unorthodox tactics, it was in this very factor that its highest recommendation lay. Biggles knew that, as well as he knew that indecision and procrastination could have but one ending, and upon his judgement in this respect he was prepared to risk all.

It was not remarkable that all eyes were on the heavy gun, and the ill-assorted team working on it, when he made his dash. What was inside the wireless hut may have offered food for speculation, but the exterior presented no attraction, so of the two subjects the gun offered most entertainment. Which again was all to Biggles's advantage, and he actually reached the machine-gun before he was seen. In the twinkling of an eye he had swung the ribbed water-jacket surrounding the muzzle in the opposite direction and squatted down behind it, thumbs on the double-thumbpiece. There was no need to take aim. The target was large and the range point-blank. Jabbing yellow flames leapt from the muzzle, and before the stream of lead the crowd disappeared like a waft of smoke in a high wind. Those who had been hit lay where they had fallen; the others raced for cover.

Biggles did not confine his attention entirely to the main body of the enemy. From time to time he slewed the barrel round and raked the surrounding rocks behind which the spectators had taken cover, and the scream of ricochetting bullets seemed to intensify the volume of fire. Suddenly the noise broke off short, and he knew that the belt was exhausted.

'Come on,' he yelled to Ginger, who was crouching behind him, automatic in hand, and made a dash for the jungle not a score of paces distant. Ginger followed. So completely successful had the sortie been that he did not have to fire a single shot during the whole engagement.

Chapter 17
Just Retribution

For a short distance they followed a narrow path through the bush, but then, knowing that they would be pursued by the Dyaks, who, at home in such surroundings, would soon overtake them, Biggles turned aside into the rank vegetation, taking care not to leave any marks that would betray them. Ginger, feeling with a queer sense of unreality that the clock had been put back a few years and he was once more playing at Indians, followed his example.

Within the forest a dim grey twilight still persisted, for the matted tree-tops met over their heads, shutting out the sunlight, while below, the secondary growth made the going difficult, and the only way they could keep moving was by constantly changing direction, taking the least obstructed path that offered itself. After the recent noise and commotion, it all seemed very still and quiet, but Biggles was not deceived; he knew that somewhere not far away the enemy would be seeking them.

Ginger realized suddenly that they were out of the trap—or nearly out—and so swiftly had the situation changed that he had difficulty in believing it. 'Where are you making for?' he whispered.

'So far, I haven't been making for anywhere in particular,' answered Biggles quietly. 'I've been quite happy to go anywhere. But now we must try to get down to the beach; I only pray that Algy is still sitting tight behind the islet. If he's had to move—but let's not think about that. Come on, let's keep going. Hello! What's that? Listen!'

From somewhere not far behind them a wild shout had echoed through the trees, to be followed immediately by others, and the swish of undergrowth.

Biggles knew what it meant. The Dyaks had found their trail and were in hot pursuit. 'Come on,' he whispered. 'It's no use trying to move without leaving a trail in this stuff; it has got to be a matter of speed.'

Neither of them will ever forget the next ten minutes. At first they tried to move quietly, but it was impossible, and in a short time they had abandoned such methods and were making all the speed possible, regardless of noise. The stagnant air, combined with the flies that rose from the foetid ground and followed them in an ever-increasing cloud, did nothing to make their progress easier, and to Ginger the flight had soon resolved itself into a delirium of whirling branches and swaying palm-fronds; but he kept his eyes on Biggles's back and followed closely on his heels. Once they plunged through a mire in which several crocodiles were wallowing, but the creatures were evidently as startled as they were, for they crashed into the bushes, leaving the way clear. On the far side the ground sloped steeply down towards the sea, the deep blue of which they could now see from time to time through the foliage. Down towards it they plunged, slipping, sliding, falling, and sometimes rolling, grabbing at any handhold to steady themselves. Occasionally they heard crashes in the bush perilously close behind them.

They burst out of the forest at a point which Biggles recognized at once; it was a little to one side of the quicksands, fortunately the side nearer to their own bay. A few hundred yards to the right the gaunt uprights of the elevated cemetery straddled the rocks near the edge of the cliff, and as they swung towards them Biggles grabbed Ginger's arm with his right hand, pointing to seaward with his left.

'Great Heavens! What on earth is all that?' he gasped.

He need not have pointed, for Ginger had already seen them—a dozen or more machines in arrowhead formation, the point directed towards the island.

'They're Vildebeests!' he yelled exultantly, as he saw the blunt noses and queerly humped backs of the aircraft. 'How the—where the—?'

'Never mind how they got here, keep going,' panted Biggles, snatching a glance over his shoulder just as the Dyaks began to stream out of the jungle. They raised a shout as they viewed their quarry.

To Biggles, the appearance of the R.A.F. machines was as miraculous as it had been to Ginger, for it was quite certain that they could not have come from Singapore in the hour that had elapsed since they had signalled the *Seafret*; but there was no time to ponder the mystery. The Dyaks were gaining on them. They were not more than fifty yards behind, and the beach was still nearly a quarter of a mile away.

As they reached the cemetery, a *kris* flashed past Biggles's shoulder and glanced off the rocks in front of him, and he knew that to continue running was to court disaster, for the next one might bury itself in his back—or Ginger's. Subconsciously he was aware of the Vildebeests nosing down towards the centre of the island, the roar of their engines drowning all other sounds, and he knew that whatever happened now their mission had been successful. In a sort of savage exultation he drew his automatic and whirled round. *Bang! Bang! Bang!* it spat as he opened rapid fire on the mob.

Bang! Bang! Bang! Ginger's gun took up the story.

The Dyaks, who were evidently well acquainted with firearms, split up like a covey of partridges going down a line of guns as they dodged for cover, and at that moment the first bomb burst.

Biggles grabbed Ginger by the arm and sped on, satisfied with the brief respite they had gained. With the roar of bursting bombs in their ears, they reached the place where the rocks sloped down to the bay, and Ginger let out a yell as the *Nemesis* came into view, her metal propellers two flashing arcs of living fire as she skimmed across the surface of the water towards them. They saw her nose turn in towards the shore and then swing out again as her keel touched the sandy bottom near the beach; saw the propellers slow down; saw Algy jump up in the cockpit and dive into the cabin, to reappear with the machine-gun, which he balanced on the windscreen. But that was all they saw for, at that moment, the whole island seemed to blow up.

Ginger afterwards swore that the ground lifted several inches under his feet, and Biggles admitted that he had never heard anything quite like it, not even during the war, although the explosion must have been similar to that of the famous Bailleul ammunition dump. It was just like a tremendous roar of thunder that went on for a full minute.

The force of it threw both Biggles and Ginger off their feet, and they finished the last twenty yards of the slope in something between a roll and a slide. And, as he lay on his back at the bottom, with the extraordinary vividness that such moments sometimes produce, a picture was printed indelibly on Ginger's brain. It was of a Vildebeest, against a background of blue sky, soaring vertically upwards and whirling like a dead leaf in a gale as the pilot strove to control his machine in such an up-current as would seldom, if ever, be encountered in nature.

Shaken, and not a little dazed, Ginger picked himself up and obeyed Biggles's order to get to the amphibian. Biggles himself, gun in hand, was looking back up the slope at the place where the Dyaks might be expected to appear. But they did not come, and presently he followed Ginger to the *Nemesis*.

Algy looked at him askance. 'If sounds are anything to go by, you *have* been having a lovely time,' he observed.

'Not so bad,' grinned Biggles. 'Where in thunder did all this aviation start from?'

Algy shrugged his shoulders. 'Don't ask me,' he answered shortly. 'I know no more about it than you do. I—' He broke off with a puzzled expression on his face, staring over Biggles's shoulder at the jungle-clad hill-side.

Ginger, following his gaze, saw a curious sight. From the centre of the island there seemed to be rising a pale green transparent cloud that writhed and coiled like a Scotch mist on an October day, and rolled in slow, turgid waves down the hill-side towards the sea. And as it rolled, and in silence embraced the forest, the foliage of the trees changed colour. The dark green of the casuarinas turned to yellow, and the emerald of the palm crests to dingy white.

As Biggles beheld this phenomenon he turned very pale and shouted one word. It was enough. The word was 'Gas', and almost before the word had died on his lips the three of them were falling into their places in the aircraft faster than they had ever embarked in all their travels.

Within a minute the *Nemesis* was tearing across the water, flinging behind her a line of swirling foam. The line ended abruptly as Biggles lifted her from the sea, and climbed slowly away from where the Vildebeests were now re-forming.

'Where to?' asked Algy.

'I think we might as well go home,' answered Biggles, glancing down through the green miasma at the flagging desolation of what had, a few minutes before, been a living forest. 'But before we do that we had better have a word or two with Sullivan,' he added, turning the nose of the *Nemesis* in the direction of Hastings Island.

Twenty minutes later he landed in the anchorage that had proved so ill-chosen for the *Seafret*, and taxied up to the beach near the stranded destroyer, where the ship's officers awaited them in a little group. From the far distance the drone of many engines rose and fell on the gentle breeze, and as he stepped ashore Biggles could see the formation of Vildebeests heading towards the island. He raised a finger and pointed to them, at the same time turning to the commander of the *Seafret*.

'Sullivan,' he said, 'can you satisfy my burning curiosity by telling me just how it happened that these aeroplanes arrived at this particular spot so opportunely?'

The commander smiled. 'That's easy,' he answered. 'I fetched them here.'

'*You* did?'

'Of course. You didn't suppose it was a fluke, did you?'

Biggles scratched his head. 'I didn't know what to think, and that's a fact,' he confessed. 'You certainly had a brain-wave. What caused it?'

'The simple fact that Lacey didn't return. I don't mind telling you that it got me all hot and bothered. It seemed to be the last straw, our only mobile unit going west—as I thought. In the circumstances there was only one thing left for me to do, which was to get in touch with R.A.F. headquarters at Singapore and ask for assistance both for myself and you. We'd got to get away from here some time, and I didn't feel like abandoning you without a search. Squadron-Leader Gore-Alliston has just landed here with his pack of airhounds, and I was just telling him the story when your message came through. Naturally, Gore-Alliston took off at once for Elephant Island. I hope he did his stuff all right.'

'He certainly did,' agreed Biggles gravely. 'There isn't a living creature left on the island, I'll warrant—human being, crocodile, or mosquito.'

Sullivan's face expressed incredulity.

'They're gassed, the lot of them,' explained Biggles. 'I didn't know our fellows carried gas-bombs nowadays—'

'Who told you they did?'

'It looks mighty like it to me.'

Sullivan shook his head. 'You've got it all wrong,' he said, 'but I can hazard a guess as to what happened. The Vildebeests were carrying ordinary hundred-and-twelve pound high explosive bombs, and they must have hit the enemy's gas-shell dump.'

'Gas-shells? Where did you get that idea?'

'When we brought the "mouldy" aboard from the junk, my gunnery officer thought it would be a good thing to have a shell or two as well, to try and find out the name of the firm who was supplying them. He tells me that they are all gas-shells—at least, all those he brought aboard the *Seafret*.'

'Jumping crocodiles! Do you mean to tell me that those skunks were going to use gas-shells if it came to a scrap?'

Sullivan nodded grimly. 'I don't suppose they were going to use them for ballast,' he observed harshly.

'Then it serves them jolly well right that they've got hoisted with their own blinking petard,' declared Biggles savagely. 'There seems to be a bit of poetic justice about what has happened that meets with my entire approval.' He turned to watch the Vildebeests land on the bay.

'What are you going to do now?' asked Sullivan.

Biggles glanced over his shoulder. 'I suppose they're sending a ship from Singapore to pick you up?' he asked.

'Yes, a destroyer is on the way.'

'In that case I'm going to hit the breeze for home,' Biggles told him. 'The people who sent us out on this jaunt will be anxious to know what is happening, and I don't think it would be wise to entrust such delicate information to ordinary lines of communication.'

'You're not going without telling us what happened on the island,' protested Sullivan.

Biggles looked pained. 'My dear chap, I wouldn't dream of doing such a thing,' he answered. 'How about a quiet bit of dinner to-night to celebrate the occasion? I can tell you all about it then.'

In Passing

Ten days later, early in the evening, the door of the sitting-room in Biggles's flat opened and Biggles walked in. He glanced at Algy and Ginger, who looked as though they had been expecting him, lit a cigarette, and flicked the dead match into the grate.

'Well, come on, out with it,' growled Ginger. 'What did he say?'

Biggles frowned. 'You mustn't call the Foreign Secretary a "he".'

'I'll call you something worse than that if you don't tell me what he said,' grinned Ginger.

'Very well, since you must know, he said, "Thank you!" '

Ginger blinked. 'He said *what*?'

' "Thank you!" Or, to be absolutely accurate, he said, "Thank you very much".'

'Is that all?'

'What did you expect? Did you suppose he was going to kiss me?'

'No, but—do you mean to tell me that was all he had to say, after all we've done?'

'Unless he wrote a song and dance about it, there isn't much more he could say, when you come to think about it, is there?'

'No, I suppose there isn't. But he might have done something—given us a gold watch apiece, for instance.'

Biggles shook his head. 'The government doesn't express its thanks by doling out gold watches,' he answered seriously. 'And, anyway, you've got something better than that. Your name is down on the Imperial archives for having rendered the state a signal service, and one day that may stand you in very good stead. When you've worked for the government as long as I have you'll know that virtue is expected to be its own reward.'

'Well, if that's all, we might as well go out and buy ourselves a bite of dinner,' declared Algy, rising.

'No need to do that,' replied Biggles, smiling. 'Lord Lottison has been kind enough to ask us all to dine with him, at his house, in order that certain members of the Cabinet may learn at first hand just what transpired during the operations of His Majesty's aircraft *Nemesis* in the Straits of the Mergui Archipelago. Go and put on your best bibs and tuckers, and look sharp about it; Cabinet Ministers don't like being kept waiting.'

Chocks Away with Biggles!

Red Fox are proud to reissue a collection of some of Captain W. E. Johns' most exciting and fast-paced stories about the flying Ace, in brand-new editions, guaranteed to entertain young and old readers alike.

BIGGLES LEARNS TO FLY
ISBN 0 09 999740 1 £3.99

BIGGLES IN FRANCE
ISBN 0 09 928311 5 £3.99

BIGGLES IN THE CAMELS ARE COMING
ISBN 0 09 928321 2 £3.99

BIGGLES AND THE RESCUE FLIGHT
ISBN 0 09 993860 X £3.99

BIGGLES OF THE FIGHTER SQUADRON
ISBN 0 09 993870 7 £3.99

BIGGLES FLIES EAST
ISBN 0 09 993780 8 £3.99

BIGGLES & CO.
ISBN 0 09 993800 6 £3.99

BIGGLES IN SPAIN
ISBN 0 09 913441 1 £3.99

BIGGLES DEFIES THE SWASTIKA
ISBN 0 09 993790 5 £3.99

BIGGLES IN THE ORIENT
ISBN 0 09 913461 6 £3.99

BIGGLES DEFENDS THE DESERT
ISBN 0 09 993840 5 £3.99

BIGGLES FAILS TO RETURN
ISBN 0 09 993850 2 £3.99

BIGGLES: SPITFIRE PARADE – a Biggles graphic novel
ISBN 0 09 930105 9 £3.99